Susie's Shoesies

Some dreams really do come true!

7/22/16

To Poppy—
    May all your
dreams come true!

    Sue Levine

Sue Madway Levine, Ed.D.

For information, contact
THINGAMAJIG, INC.
411 Lilac Drive
Kennett Square, PA 19348

ISBN-10: 0615426867
ISBN-13: 9780615426860

Dedication

To Stan, who taught me how beautiful and easy life can be; to my boys, whose creativity, intelligence, and loving nature inspire me and keep me reading great literature; to grandmothers, who teach real life lessons to their grandchildren; and to all the Susies who *stand up* rather than *stand by*.

Table of Contents

Become a Strategic Reader

You are about to begin a wonderful journey. Excitement and adventure are just a few pages away as you begin reading this first book in the *Susie's Shoesies* series.

Reading is not just saying words or hearing them read to you. Reading is a search for meaning…a way for you to share other people's thoughts and experiences and grow the meaning of your own life.

To get the most out of a reading experience, there are things good readers do that make themselves better readers who are better able to understand and remember what they have read. Looking at the title and cover of a book can give you clues as to what a book is about, who the characters are, and where the story takes place.

So good readers have questions about a book even **before** they read the first page. Once they start reading, new questions come up **during** the reading itself. As they finish a chapter, new thoughts emerge, and good readers ask themselves questions **after** reading like "I wonder what will happen next?"

Look at the cover of *Susie's Shoesies*. Let's start with the title. What does the title make you think the book is about? As you look at the drawing, who do you think is the main character of this book? Where do you think the main character lives? How old do you think the main character is? What kind of a person is the main character? What do you think is one of the main character's favorite things to eat? Now start reading and see if you were right!

There is a surprise recipe at the end of the book. You and your friends and family can make it just like the characters in this book. Yummy, yummy! What do you think will come out of your oven once you have followed the recipe?

For more information about this book and its characters, please go to the *Susie's Shoesies* website, www. SusiesShoesies.com. There you can actually hear the author read the book to you, and you can learn more about how this story was created.

If you are interested in becoming the best reader you can be, you can find **before, during,** and **after** questions, to guide your understanding of the story, at the back of this book. Please pay attention to which questions are meant to be discussed before reading, which during reading, and which are meant to be left for after you've read a particular chapter. If you get ahead of yourself, you may ruin surprises that are meant to be exciting and mystifying.

Make sure you have read a few pages of each chapter before you read the **during** questions...and finish the chapter before looking at the **after** questions. This will allow you to have the most fun and the best experience with this book. You and your friends and family can download and discuss them as a part of your own book club. With a little hot chocolate and a piece of you-know-what, you can enjoy this book and the other books in the *Susie's Shoesies* series that will follow.

Prologue

December 10, 1948

"Madam Chairman, how proud are you to have gathered all the delegates in support of your committee's recommendations today? Surely this historic occasion is one of your most stunning accomplishments," the *New York Times* reporter asked.

"Since the spring of 1946, when our noble president saw fit to appoint me to the position of the United States Representative to the General Assembly of the United Nations, it has been quite challenging work to lead that esteemed body's Human Rights Commission," the former First Lady replied. "And now that our Universal Declaration of Human Rights has been adopted, I do not for one minute believe our work is completed. There is still much to do if we are to protect the rights of all men and women across the world."

"I have long admired your willingness, as the longest-serving First Lady in our country's history, to speak out on behalf of the common man," the reporter added. "You have advocated for the rights of women and children, championed civil rights for all oppressed peoples, and had the confidence to disagree with your late husband when your values were being underrepresented. And I have fervently looked forward to reading your syndicated writing. Are you aware that your six-day-a-week 'My Day' column is carried by ninety newspapers across the nation, and your opinions are read by more than four million people?"

"Thank you for your kind words, Brandon. I'm certain this forum for my positions has influenced both national and world opinion…which may have contributed to today's historic outcome. The fact that our commission's point of view has been so enthusiastically embraced by the United Nations delegates gives me hope that their mother nations will enact laws, amend their constitutions, and put other policies into effect to make our document a reality."

"Any regrets along the way?" the reporter queried.

"I'm sure you are aware of the rift between my uncle Teddy and the other branch of his family; my late husband so admired Theodore, and yet their political differences and approaches collided from time to time over the years. To answer your question, I would say that, if it were possible, I would love to see the broad, smiling face of my uncle once again, now that I have come into my own and championed the causes he so respected. I do regret his not being with me at this time."

"Although he is not family, President Truman appears to be one of your staunchest supporters. He certainly concurs with your approach to social justice issues, so perhaps knowing that three presidents have touted your vision and passion for human dignity will fill the void that exists, now that the presidential cousins have passed on," the respectful reporter suggested.

"Truth be told, I have never been one to look for approval from others. Neither my mother nor grandmother offered much in the way of emotional support or encouragement, so I learned to rely on my own opinions and understanding of issues I found important. I believe my education led to my sense of self and propelled me toward a future of public service. And while I have great respect and admiration for my late husband, as he did for me, there was just something exhilarating about being around Teddy that made my world a better place. I miss him very much," she added.

"The attitude that shaped my decisions might be a little shocking for your readers, young man, but you may as well quote this sentiment in your article: I believe you must do what you feel in your heart to be right, for you'll be criticized anyway. You'll be damned if you do and damned if you don't. So we must have the self-confidence to stand up and speak up to be heard above the fray."

It was this approach that drove "the First Lady of the world," as President Truman referred to her, to a lifetime of service. She was the first wife of a sitting president to speak at a nominating convention, and her address on July 18, 1940, rallied the Democratic Party and the nation to reelect her husband for a third term as president while much of the world was at war. Known as the "no ordinary time" speech, she inspired the nation to embrace her steadfast belief that

> No man who is a candidate or who is president can carry this situation alone. This is only carried by a united people who love their country and who will live for it to the fullest of their ability with the highest of ideals, with a determination that their party shall be absolutely devoted to the good of the nation as a whole and to doing what this country can to bring the world to a safer and happier condition.

She remained the chair of the Human Rights Commission until 1956 and then was appointed chair of the John F. Kennedy administration's Presidential Commission on the Status of Women. When Eleanor Roosevelt died on November 7, 1962, at the age of 78, her obituary in the *New York Times* referred to her as "the object of almost universal respect."

CHAPTER ONE

A Special Visitor

From the moment she woke up, Susie Gardner had a feeling December 9, 2007, would turn out to be an extraordinary day. There was something in the air, something even more special than the winter's first snowfall or the sweet smell of burning oak logs wafting up through the chimneys of homes trying to take the chill out of a cold day.

As she walked home from school and approached her house on Lafayette Road, Susie thought she noticed a familiar smell. When she opened the kitchen door, she knew for sure. The sweet aroma of her mom's chewy, gooey, dark chocolate fudge cake filled the air.

This could mean only one thing; Granny Ella was coming to visit. Susie's mom only made the chewy, gooey, dark chocolate fudge cake when her own mother, Susie's granny, came to visit. Granny Ella had come to expect her favorite cake to be waiting for her. This time her arrival was part of a very special occasion...a very special occasion times two.

Susie and her grandmother had a remarkable relationship. Of all the people in her family, it was her granny who really understood her. She knew what Susie was thinking even without Susie saying a word. They laughed at the same kind of jokes, liked the same kind of movies, and were inspired by the same kind of people and events. They were two of a kind.

After hugging her mother and confirming her hunch that Granny Ella was on her way, Susie ran to her room to tidy up for her grandmother's arrival. Granny Ella always slept in the other twin bed in Susie's room. That was the best part…staying up late and discussing wondrous ideas, listening to stories about her granny's childhood, and waking up early the next morning to hear more about the amazing life her grandmother had led.

As Susie emptied out a drawer in her dresser, to make room for Granny Ella's belongings, she picked up one of the pictures she kept next to her jewelry box. It was a photo of her grandmother taken when she was eight years old. Today's visit was perfect timing; tomorrow, December 10, 2007, was Susie's eighth birthday, and she was so excited to know her granny was coming all the way from Greensburg, Pennsylvania, to be with her on her special day. But it wasn't just Susie's special day; December tenth was also her grandmother's birthday. They had been born exactly seventy-five years apart.

As Susie looked at the picture, she could hear her dad saying, "You look just like your granny did when she was your age." When she looked at her grandmother's long, curly, blond hair, full lips, big smile, and sparkling blue eyes, Susie might as well have been looking at herself in the mirror.

There was another picture of Granny Ella on the nightstand next to Susie's bed. In this one, her grandmother was a young woman. Although Susie did not know where the picture had been taken, Granny Ella was looking up at the camera surrounded by what appeared to be several of her friends. But her resemblance to Susie was still easy to see. When Susie looked at this picture, it was like a glimpse into her own future, a picture of what she, Susie, would look like when she became a young woman.

Susie's life as a soon-to-be eight-year-old was very different from her granny's childhood. Granny Ella had been raised on a turkey farm in Kiev, Russia, where there were hours of chores to complete every day, rain or snow, all year round.

Ella Medavoy was one of eight children. She had three older brothers and four younger sisters. Grandmother Didi also lived on the farm with Ella's mother and father, Mary and Ruben Medavoy.

Granny Ella was seven years old when she came with her mother, Grandma Didi, and her brothers and sisters to America by boat. Granny Ella's father was already settled in Pittsburgh, Pennsylvania, when he sent for the rest of his family. Some of the best stories Granny Ella told were about their ten-day voyage to America.

Although none of the Medavoy children had gone to school in Russia, they all learned English quickly when they came to America and attended school in their new neighborhood. They were wise beyond their young years and had learned life lessons that could not be taught in a classroom. Because they looked so much alike, when Susie looked at the pictures her granny had saved over the years, she felt as if she were living in her grandmother's shoes.

CHAPTER TWO

A Present for Susie

After dinner, as Susie was finishing making room for Granny Ella's clothes in her bedroom, she heard her seven-year-old brother, Bennett, squeal, "Granny's here! She's very near! Ella Bella has come from far away to stay. And it looks like she has a birthday present for Susie!"

Susie laughed at her brother's way of announcing their granny's arrival. This was a new phase he was going through, speaking in rhyme.

Susie was the perfect big sister, and her relationship with Bennett was more than the typical brother-and-sister kind. They were friends. They played together. They had fun together and sometimes got into trouble together too. And even though they each had their own bedroom, Bennett often slept in the other twin bed in Susie's room—especially since the accident.

Last spring, when Bennett was six years old, he ran across the street after Jackie, the family dog. He did not look before he darted out. Although Jackie made it safely across the road, a passing car struck Bennett. His left leg was badly crushed, but everyone was relieved a broken leg was his most serious physical injury. However, his emotional scars were just as serious and went mostly un-detected…by everyone but Susie.

After two operations and three months in a cast, Bennett was able to walk again. But six months later, he was still unable to move as quickly as he could before the accident. Susie noticed he seemed less confident, and she often heard him crying out in his sleep. To hide his fears, Bennett became something of a comedian, making jokes and playing pranks on family members and friends. Everyone was amazed by how resilient he was. And while he had been very brave through all of the physical pain, hospital stays, and physical therapy sessions, Susie knew his behavior, including speaking in rhyme, was his attempt at hiding his disappointments. He was comforted by all of the attention he got while his leg was healing, and now his comedic behavior continued to make him the center of attention long after his leg was healed.

Susie tried very hard to be patient, not only with her brother, but also with the rest of her family and their reaction to Bennett's injuries. It was not an easy time for her, either. She missed the way her family used to be when they would rush out and about, going to the park or shopping, or to the movies. But after the accident, everyone seemed to be walking on eggshells, and there was less time for the fun things they used to do.

It was not that Susie was jealous of all the attention her young brother was getting; she just missed the attention that used to come her way. At times, she felt left out. But at night, when Bennett would knock on her bedroom door with his pillow in his arms, she knew he felt most comfortable in the company of his big sister, and she felt proud.

Two nights ago, her mother came into Susie's room and found Bennett fast asleep in the other bed. Susie had still been awake reading when her mother bent down and kissed her good night. And when she thanked Susie for being such a wonderful sister and daughter, Susie felt even prouder. Her mother promised her life was going to return to normal. Susie laughed and said to her mom, "But normal would be boring!"

To that her mother replied, "Well, there are some surprises coming your way. Remember, in three days it will be our very special little girl's very special eighth birthday."

That day was almost here, and best of all, Granny Ella had just arrived.

Susie ran down the hall, down the stairs, and almost ran right into her granny, who was starting up the stairs to find her. It had been a year since they last saw each other. As Granny Ella reached up to hug Susie, she said, "I swear you have grown a foot since my last visit!"

Susie thought her granny looked a little different too…a little more tired, and there was maybe a little more gray in her curls. Her grandmother also looked a little shorter, or was it that Susie was a little taller? In any case, Granny Ella still had that twinkle in her eye, her wide smile, and bright red lipstick that were her trademark. Her hug was just as warm, just as gentle, and just as comforting as ever.

Granny Ella bent down and protectively picked up a gift-wrapped box she had placed on the bottom step when she saw Susie bounding down the stairs. As Susie brought her grandmother's small suitcase up the steps, she kept an eye on the box that Granny Ella was carrying.

It was just about bedtime once Granny Ella had finished unpacking. Susie went into the bathroom to wash and get ready for bed, and when she came out, dressed in her favorite flannel pajamas, the package her granny had been carrying was sitting next to Susie's pillow. Susie tried to control her curiosity and excitement as she picked up the box.

"Is this for me?" she asked.

Her granny smiled at her. "This is the most special birthday present I have ever given you, my dear first granddaughter. It is something for you to wear tomorrow on your birthday. But I want you to open it now, so I can tell you all about it before the excitement of our big day begins."

Susie carefully untied the lovely white bow and undid the beautiful red-and-pink wrapping paper. Although the box gave no hint of what was inside, Susie was careful not to shake it for fear of breaking something so special.

As she gently lifted the lid off the box and pushed aside the top layer of tissue paper, Susie was left breathless at the sight of her granny's present. Inside the box was a pair of the most beautiful shoes Susie had ever seen. They were bright red, the color of her granny's lips, and completely covered in red sequins. They seemed to glow as if they were electrified and shone so brightly that Susie was not sure if she should even touch them.

Granny Ella said, "Do you like them, sweetheart?"

Susie hugged the box close to her chest and looked up at her grandmother. "They are the most amazingly beautiful shoes I have ever seen! Are they really for me? Can I put them on right now?"

Her grandmother stood up from the bed, lifted them out of the box, and carefully put them on Susie's feet. All at once, the most wonderful and unexpected feeling of warmth and joy raced from Susie's toes, up her legs, past her tummy, and straight to her heart. She stood up and hugged her granny so tightly that they both fell back onto the bed, laughing and giggling.

Susie said, "Granny, where did you find these? I have never seen anything like them in any store."

To that her grandmother replied, "I did not buy them…I am passing them down to you. You see Susie, my grandmother, Didi, gave them to me, her first grand-daughter, seventy-five years ago, on *my* eighth birthday, the year after we came to America. I have saved them for a moment like this, to give these very special shoes to my very special first granddaughter. Now I know what joy my grandmother must have felt when she gave them to me all those years ago."

Granny Ella told Susie the story of the day she received the shoes. Their family had been very poor, both when they lived in Russia and especially during those first few years after they moved to America. "My mother, Mary, was a seamstress and took clothes in and let them out to fit whoever needed them at the moment. Although I never had new clothes or anything that was bought just for me, it did not make me sad. In fact, I actually felt lucky to have so many of my family's clothes to choose from over the years.

"However, on the night before my eighth birthday, Grandmother Didi came into my bedroom with a special box under her arm. She hugged me and said she was giving me a very special birthday gift she had bought several years before from a *shaman* back in Russia. He was known to possess magical powers and told her if she gave them to me, her first granddaughter, on my eighth birthday, the shoes would bring me good luck and good fortune whenever I put them on."

Susie had stretched out on top of her covers as she listened to her grandmother's story. Granny Ella noticed Susie was still wearing the new shoes and was sure it would do no good to suggest Susie take them off. The red glow of the beautiful gift seemed to wrap itself around her granddaughter, and Granny Ella did not want to disrupt the magic that seemed to fill the room.

Just then, the door to Susie's bedroom came crashing open and in rushed her brother, Bennett. He stopped suddenly and quizzically looked around, trying to find the source of the red glow that was flowing into the hall from under Susie's bedroom door. "Ella Bella...Susie...what's going on? Is there a fire? Everything is so...RED!"

"Bennett, come see what Granny gave me for my birthday!"

Her brother walked over to the side of Susie's bed and asked, "Where did you find those, Ella Bella?" Susie told him the story of their grandmother's red shoes.

Bennett could not contain himself. He ran out into the hall and shouted to his mother and father, "Everyone come here, come here. Come see Susie's new shoesies."

Susie's mom was the first to enter her room. She was carrying a tray, and when Granny Ella saw her, she said, "I thought you might have forgotten. Is that my favorite bedtime snack?"

When Susie's mom put the tray down on her grandmother's bed, Susie and Granny Ella smiled at each other. There were two plates, two forks, two glasses of milk, and two pieces of the chewy, gooey, dark chocolate fudge cake.

As Susie and her grandmother began eating their delicious chocolate treat, her mom smiled knowingly at her own mother. "You finally gave them to her. They are just lovely, Mom." When Susie's father came in, he too seemed to know this was a gift that would someday come to his daughter. Susie's parents hugged each other and then embraced Granny Ella.

Then Susie's mother reminded everyone that tomorrow was a big day, and they should all try to go to sleep—although she knew her daughter would be too excited to settle into slumber right away. She bent down to kiss Susie goodnight and started to remove her daughter's new shoes. Susie begged her mom to let her wear them a little longer and her mother said, "OK, as long as you are sure to take them off before you go to sleep."

"Of course I will," Susie said. "Who would wear shoes to bed?"

Susie's mother then went over to her own mother's bedside and gave her a gentle kiss on her warm cheek. "Thanks, Mom," she said as their eyes met in a knowing way. She stood there a moment longer, looking lovingly and somewhat longingly at these two very special, curly-haired members of her family.

Susie noticed both her mother and Granny Ella had tears in their eyes. "What's wrong?" Susie said with fear in her heart.

Her mother looked back at her and smiled, just as a tear ran down her cheek. "I am so happy to share this moment with my two favorite girls. I have a feeling your birthdays are going to be very special this year." And with that, Susie's mom turned off the light on the nightstand and looked back at the red glow she knew would never fade from her daughter's life.

CHAPTER THREE

A Problem in the Neighborhood

As was their tradition, Susie and Granny Ella lay in bed and talked about what was going on in their lives as they drifted off to sleep. Susie was happy to have this alone time with her grandmother. She always found Granny Ella to have wonderful insights into the things that were important to her. Because her grandmother had seen so much of life and had been to so many unusual and amazing places, Susie knew she could ask her granny anything and get a fascinating story in response.

Susie liked that Granny Ella never told her what to do or what to think. However, her grandmother had an interesting habit of asking lots of questions that made Susie think about things differently.

So Susie was not surprised when her granny said, "Sweetheart, how has your school year been going?"

Even if Granny Ella hadn't asked, Susie was going to tell her about a very special report she had written that she knew her grandmother would find most interesting.

"Oh, Granny, I have spent a lot of time learning about Eleanor Roosevelt...President Franklin D. Roosevelt's wife. What an amazing woman she was. Did you ever meet her?"

Granny Ella smiled and said, "I never got to meet her, but the picture you have of me on your nightstand with my friends was taken in 1948, after we heard Mrs. Roosevelt speak at a very famous meeting in Paris, France. She really changed the role of First Ladies in our country. Those women who followed in her footsteps tried to do more than just look beautiful standing next to their presidential husbands."

Susie was not surprised that her grandmother seemed to know so much about Mrs. Roosevelt. She asked Granny Ella, "Did you know that Mrs. Roosevelt resigned from one of the most famous organizations in the country, the Daughters of the American Revolution, because they would not allow Marian Anderson to sing at one of their meetings...just because she was an African American? That's discrimination, and now it's against the law because of people like Eleanor Roosevelt."

"You're right, Susie. And did you know that when they refused to allow Mrs. Anderson to sing at Constitution Hall, right here in Philadelphia, Mrs. Roosevelt arranged for her to sing in front of the Lincoln Memorial in Washington, DC, on Easter Sunday of that same year. Thousands more people got to hear her beautiful voice than would have if she had sung in Philadelphia. So in the end, things worked out in an amazing way.

"After the disgraceful incident with Marian Anderson, I remember listening to the radio and hearing Mrs. Roosevelt say, 'No one can make you feel inferior without your consent.' Eleanor Roosevelt's actions during the thirties and forties inspired many people to stand up for their rights."

This reminded Susie of something that had recently upset one of her friends. "Wait till you hear this, Granny. After I read my report in class, Lois Bernstein rushed over to me at the lunch table. She told me that her family wanted to join the Wynnehall Country Club, where we belong, and they were turned down! Her father told her it was because they were Jewish and that no Jewish people were allowed to belong to the club. I can't believe it… right here in America! Right here in Merion, Pennsylvania!

"Last year in history class we learned the founding fathers of our country came to America for religious freedom. They wanted the new land to welcome all kinds of people and make it possible for them to worship however they wanted. I also learned the Statue of Liberty is a symbol of that freedom, and people who have come to America from all over the world, like your family, Granny Ella, have been greeted in New York City harbor by her promise of liberty. My teacher called it 'an appreciation of diversity,' and it is part of what makes our country so great. For my friend's family to have these problems is like taking a giant step back in time. It made me so angry! When I told my dad, he said he was going to look into it."

"What do you think should be done if your dad finds out this is true?" her grandmother asked. "Do you think being angry will make a difference? Eleanor Roosevelt once said, 'It's better to light a candle than to curse the darkness.'"

"That is such an amazing thing to think about. Sitting around being upset probably won't accomplish anything," Susie said. "I bet if Eleanor Roosevelt were here, she would know what to do. I would love to be able to talk to her about this. If she were still alive, I would write to her. One thing I do know," Susie said. "If my friend isn't good enough for Wynnehall Country Club, then that club isn't good enough for me! I will never go there again, and they will lose the best swimmer on their swim team."

A smile filled Granny Ella's face as she said, "I'm so proud of you, sweetheart." She continued to think about the stand her granddaughter was taking as the glow of the red shoes continued to light up the room. Granny Ella told Susie, "Just like Eleanor Roosevelt, I have always admired women who questioned things that did not make sense or seemed unfair. Even though speaking out about things we feel are wrong might upset some people, as Mrs. Roosevelt once said, 'What is to give light must endure the burning.' You'll have to be prepared for those people who do not agree with you, my dear."

As Susie's eyes began to close, the last words she heard were those of her grandmother as she said, "Those of us who have the courage of our convictions make history, Susie." The glowing red shoes cast a comforting warmth that seemed to soothe these two special women as they began to drift off to sleep the night before their birthdays. The last thing Granny Ella remembered was that Susie had forgotten to take off her new shoes.

CHAPTER FOUR

Where Am I?

When the warmth of the sun shining through the window touched her face, Susie opened her eyes. She looked around, expecting to see her favorite posters that hung on her pink-striped wallpaper. They weren't there. She looked over to the pink-and-white bookcase next to her desk, and it wasn't there either. And where was her desk, anyway?

When Susie looked to the right, where her grandmother had gone to sleep in the twin bed next to hers, there was no Granny Ella…and no twin beds. What there was instead was a very big room with a very high ceiling. The walls were lined with books and in the center of the room was a large round wooden table, above which hung a sparkling chandelier. There was a fireplace, and over the mantel was a portrait of George Washington. What happened to her wizard and rock star posters? Susie did not recognize her bedroom. She did not even know if this was her bedroom

Just then, a tall, important-looking man in a dark blue suit stepped into the room and told Susie, "The former First Lady will be with you in just a moment. She is saying good-bye to Mrs. Truman and will meet you here in the library shortly."

The former First Lady? The library? Saying good-bye to Mrs. Truman? Susie looked around and saw she was standing in a formal-looking room with red, white, and blue curtains, chairs, and a couch. When the door opened, and Susie looked in that direction, she saw a woman who looked a lot like Eleanor Roosevelt walking toward her. As the tall and stately woman began to speak, Susie realized it really was Mrs. Roosevelt, and she was bending down to shake her hand!

"It's so wonderful to meet you, Susie," said Mrs. Roosevelt. "When I received your letter, I told Betty Idstein, my personal secretary, to get in touch with you right away. I wanted to try to help you and your friends with this problem in your neighborhood. You are just as lovely as your letter, but a bit taller than I would have thought an almost eight-year-old would be. And look at those beautiful red shoes. Where did you get them?"

"Oh, Mrs. Roosevelt! I am so excited to meet you. Thank you so much for inviting me here to the White House. My Granny Ella once heard you speak and told me how amazing you were. She is the one who gave me my red shoes last night for my birthday. I wrote a report about you for school, and when this trouble started in my hometown, I knew you would know what to do."

"Tell me more about what has been going on, Susie."

"It all started a month ago when my best friend, Lois Bernstein, and her family wanted to join the Wynnehall Country Club. That's the club my family belongs to. Lois said they got a letter telling them they would have to be put on a waiting list because there were no openings for new members. The worst part was the letter went on to say that the Bernsteins should apply for membership at the

Overhill Country Club 'where there are many Jewish families like you and where you might feel more comfortable.'

"When we were talking about the letter at the lunch table, our other friend, Irene Baron said, 'We just applied to join Wynnehall last week, and my dad said he was told we would receive our membership cards within a few days. I am planning to have my birthday party by the club pool next month.'

"Well, Mrs. Roosevelt, it reminded me of the time Marian Anderson was not allowed to sing at Independence Hall…and you did something remarkable when people discriminated against her. My granny says, 'Women who have the courage of their convictions make history,' like you have, Mrs. Roosevelt."

"Do you think you are brave enough to speak out for what you believe in, Susie?" Mrs. Roosevelt asked. "It can be very scary to stand up to a whole group of people all by yourself."

"I'm not sure, but I will try to be. Didn't you once say, 'You must do the things you think you cannot do'? Oh, and I won't be alone. All of my friends are upset about this. We don't want any family to be treated this way. It's not fair. It's not American. Things like this are not supposed to happen any more. What do you think I can do, Mrs. Roosevelt?"

The First Lady reached out for Susie's hand and looked deeply into her eyes. "Susie, you remind me of myself. I'll bet we can come up with a plan to make history in your little town. My visit with President and Mrs. Truman is over, and I must be going. Do you have time to come with me to an important meeting I have to attend? It may give us some ideas."

Susie remembered President Truman had been the vice president when Mrs. Roosevelt's husband was president. When President Roosevelt died in 1945, the vice president became the president of the United States. Even though she was no longer the First Lady, it was obvious Mrs. Roosevelt was still very close to the Trumans and still involved in politics.

Susie was confused. How could she be in the Truman White House? Harry Truman was president in the late 1940s. Susie would have to have gone back in time to be visiting the White House during his presidency. And that wasn't possible, was it?

Just as these thoughts were beginning to worry her, the former First Lady took Susie's hand, and they left the library. Susie turned to her and said, "I can't believe I am here with you, Mrs. Roosevelt. It's so wonderful of you to care about our town and its problem. This all feels like a dream, but I know it's real; I can feel your hand in mine. I would be honored to go with you."

CHAPTER FIVE

Where Am I Going?

Susie could not believe how many men and women it took to escort one famous woman and one small child to a meeting. When they exited the White House, Susie saw that a very special car was waiting for them. She had seen limousines on television and in the movies, but this car was very different. Susie never imagined a car could be so beautiful, shiny, and enormous as the one she was heading toward. Although it looked old-fashioned, it had an elegance that could not compare to the cars back at home. There were many other important-looking cars in front of and behind what appeared to be Mrs. Roosevelt's car, and Susie couldn't help but wonder where they were going.

When Susie climbed into the car, she felt like she was entering someone's private den. The large black leather seats were soft and comfortable, and there was a small coffee table and reading lamp nearby.

Susie noticed there were several magazines and newspapers on the coffee table, and she could see one magazine had a picture of Mrs. Roosevelt on the cover. She picked it up and read the caption: "Former First Lady to address the United Nations' General Assembly on Human Rights."

Susie was confused by this and even a little scared. The date on the magazine was December 5, 1948! This had to be an old magazine, and yet it looked brand new. When Susie saw the date on the two newspapers was December 9, 1948, she became even more confused. Was it 1948? But how could that be? Susie knew her own birth date was December 10, 1999. She wasn't even born in 1948!

Mrs. Roosevelt sensed something was bothering her young friend. She put her arm around Susie's shoulder and said, "My dear child, try not to worry. I have no doubt this will be a day you will always remember, even though right now it might seem a little confusing and overwhelming."

Susie felt the sincerity and warmth of Mrs. Roosevelt's words and put her worries aside. She knew she was in the care of one of the world's most important people, who would not let any harm come to her.

All along the way, cars were pulled over, and people were watching and waving as the long Lincoln Continental Coupe with an American flag on each fender made its way along the highway. Susie felt like she was the only one who did not know what was happening.

Just then, Susie noticed the car was taking an exit marked with an airplane and an arrow. She turned to Mrs. Roosevelt and asked, "Are we going to the airport?" The former First Lady put her hand in Susie's hand, smiled, and nodded her head. Were they going there to meet someone? The only time Susie had ever been to an airport was to pick up her Uncle Andrew when he came from California to visit last Thanksgiving.

A few minutes later, the car made its way past all the check-in areas marked for the airline companies. It slowed down as it took a turn onto a road that led away from the rest of the airport traffic. They seemed to be headed toward a very large building with very, very large garage doors.

Slowly, very slowly, one of the enormous doors began to rise. Susie could see there were two shiny silver airplanes inside the building. It was then that Susie thought she understood what was about to happen.

"Are we taking a plane to your meeting?" Susie asked the former First Lady. She had never been on an airplane before and the thought of it both scared and excited her.

"Yes, Susie. We are going to fly across the Atlantic Ocean. The meeting I have to go to is in Paris, France. We will sleep on the plane tonight, and when we wake up tomorrow morning, we will be there. Do you speak any French, Susie?"

Speak French? Fly across the Atlantic Ocean? Paris, France? The farthest Susie had ever been away from home was when her family took the train to New York City to see a Broadway play.

Sleep on the plane? Susie suddenly realized she did not have a suitcase with her...no pajamas, or toothbrush, or hairbrush. And what would she wear when she woke up? The closest thing to French food Susie knew was French fries...and she wasn't sure they were even really French. And what about her parents? They were probably wondering where she was at this very minute.

Mrs. Roosevelt sensed Susie was feeling overwhelmed. She reached into her pocketbook, took out a small envelope, and handed it to Susie. "This letter came to my office for you, dear." Susie opened the envelope and immediately recognized the handwriting. It read,

My dear Susie,

I know this will be an important and magical birthday that you will always remember and treasure. I also know you are in good hands and will come back to us safely. Trust your heart and your instincts. You will know just what to do to make the most of your journey.

The letter was signed, "With love, Granny Ella." But how had her grandmother known where Susie was, and how had she gotten this letter to her? Susie had no idea.

CHAPTER SIX

Where Do Human Rights Begin?

As their car entered the large garage-like building, Susie's mind was filled with questions. Although the silver planes were shiny and looked like they could be new, at the same time they looked very old-fashioned. Susie had seen lots of airplanes on television and in movies and had watched when her Uncle Andrew's plane landed at Philadelphia Airport. The planes she was looking at now were not anything like those she had seen before.

These planes had propellers and looked like the airplanes in the old movies Susie used to watch with her Grandfather Ralphie. Were they really going to travel across the ocean in one of these airplanes?

Mrs. Roosevelt sensed Susie's concern. "Did you know that my husband, Franklin, was the first president to fly in an airplane while in office?" she said. "He flew to a very important meeting during the last world war to confer with the leaders of the countries who were fighting on our side. The plane on the right side of the hangar is the

Boeing 314 Pan American Dixie Clipper that took him there."

"What is that other plane?" Susie asked.

Mrs. Roosevelt replied, "It is another Boeing 314, the one President Truman is lending us to go to our meeting in Paris."

Susie was feeling overwhelmed. Mrs. Roosevelt looked over at her nervous young friend and said, "Susie, I packed you a suitcase before I left for my meeting at the White House. I have an eight-year-old granddaughter who is just about your size. She keeps some clothes at my house in Hyde Park for sleepovers. I'm sure she won't mind if you wear them while we are away."

That put a smile on Susie's face. Mrs. Roosevelt went on to say, "Airplanes had an enormous effect on the way World War II was fought. The Wright brothers would be shocked to see all the improvements that have been made since their first plane flew in Kitty Hawk, North Carolina."

"Boy, would they. If only they could see the jets that fly now. My science teacher explained they can fly faster than the speed of sound. The Wright brothers wouldn't believe their eyes!"

Now it was Mrs. Roosevelt who looked confused. "What is a 'jet,' my dear?" she asked. It was then Susie realized that, although it appeared she had somehow traveled back in time, Mrs. Roosevelt apparently had not been to the future.

Right then the door to the car was opened, and the former First Lady and Susie were helped out of the vehicle. Once again, Susie was amazed to see so many people gathered around them. "Are they all going on the plane to Paris with us?" she asked Mrs. Roosevelt.

"Just my secretary and one other member of the American delegation," Mrs. Roosevelt replied.

"What delegation?" Susie politely asked.

Mrs. Roosevelt explained. "I am the United States representative to the General Assembly of the United Nations. As chairman of the Human Rights Commission, I have helped to write a document called the Universal Declaration of Human Rights. It is my hope that when I present it to the General Assembly, the other delegates will accept this plan."

"Oh, I am so proud of you, Mrs. Roosevelt. Granny Ella was right. You are such an amazing woman. I am so excited to be going with you to such an important event. This really will change history, won't it?

"And speaking of change, shouldn't your title be 'chairwoman,' Mrs. Roosevelt?"

The former First Lady smiled. "I knew you would give me a fresh perspective on the issues the assembly will face. I also think these issues are similar to those you are facing in your neighborhood, Susie. What is happening in your town is exactly what we will be talking about in Paris."

Mrs. Roosevelt went on to say, "Susie, I believe that the future belongs to those who believe in their dreams. But believing in the equality of all people has been more than a dream for me; it has been my goal in life to see that all people are treated fairly and with dignity.

"People ask me where human rights begin, and I say to them, they begin in small places, close to home—so close and so small that they can not be seen on any maps of the world. Yet they are the world of the individual person—the neighborhood he lives in, the school or college he attends, the factory, farm, or office where he works. Such are the places where every man, woman, and child seeks equal justice, equal opportunity, equal dignity without discrimination.

"Susie, unless these rights have meaning there, they have little meaning anywhere. Without concerted citizen action to uphold them close to home, we shall look in vain for progress in the larger world.

"Think about this and what your friend's family is going through. As you listen to the speeches tomorrow, perhaps you will get some good ideas for your own town. With the new day comes new strength, so now we will have to rest up to be ready for the challenges of tomorrow."

"Where is the delegation meeting, Mrs. Roosevelt?" Susie asked.

"We are meeting at the Palais de Chaillot in Paris. Have you ever been in a palace, Susie?"

Susie could not believe her ears. She was going to a real palace! If only Granny Ella could be there too. Susie knew this would be something her grandmother would love to see. Susie also knew she would have to pay very close attention so she could remember every detail to tell her grandmother when she returned home. A palace! She felt like a princess as they walked toward the shiny silver plane.

CHAPTER SEVEN

Up, Up, and Away!

Susie held Mrs. Roosevelt's hand as they were led to the plane that would fly them across the ocean. The four propellers were spinning at such a high speed that Mrs. Roosevelt had to hold onto her hat, or it would have blown away.

Up the short, carpeted stairs they climbed, until they were inside the shiny airplane. There were couches, tables, and chairs, and many important-looking people treating Susie like she was someone important too. She couldn't help but notice that the hairstyles and clothes they were wearing had the same look and style as the clothes worn by Granny Ella and her friends, in the photo on Susie's nightstand back at home.

As they walked down the aisle toward what looked like a living room, Susie began to worry that the plane might be too big to fly. Although it was not fancy nor decorated like the White House or her home, it appeared to have everything needed to make the passengers comfortable on their journey across the Atlantic Ocean. The look was more like the kinds of furniture Susie saw when she went shopping in antique stores with her mom and even reminded her of Granny Ella's home in Greensburg.

Mrs. Roosevelt asked Susie, "Would you like to freshen up before dinner? There is a nice bathroom off your bedroom, and the suitcase I mentioned is waiting there for you." *A bathroom? My bedroom?* That was when Susie remembered it would take all night to get to Paris, France.

Mrs. Roosevelt's secretary walked Susie through the kitchen to the back of the plane and showed her into one of two bedrooms. Susie saw there were two twin beds, smaller than the beds in Susie's bedroom back home, and the room itself was quite small. There were no pictures or decorations on the curved walls, but the red-and-pink-flowered bedspreads and matching curtain covering the window gave the room a cozy feeling.

Just as Mrs. Roosevelt had said, there was a tan suitcase on the bed closer to the door. It had already been opened, and Susie could see it was filled with all kinds of pretty clothes any little girl would love. There was another suitcase on the other bed, and Susie realized someone else might be staying in the room with her.

Susie went into the bathroom to get washed before dinner. Hanging near the sink were the fluffiest white towels she had ever seen. Each one had a blue-and-gold emblem like the one she remembered seeing when she saw the president appear on TV. "These must be the president's towels!" Susie said to herself, almost afraid to use them.

Then Susie noticed there were two toothbrushes in the holder on the wall and two soap dishes. Yes, it did look like someone else was going to be sharing the room with her. For a moment, Susie closed her eyes and wished that Granny Ella would…could be there with her, just like at home in Merion. But Susie knew her grandmother would be so happy for her to be having such an adventure. So Susie washed up and rejoined Mrs. Roosevelt in the dining area of the airplane.

As soon as she sat down, three waiters approached to announce the choices for dinner that evening. Choices? This was like eating at a restaurant. Susie said she would like a hamburger and French fries while Mrs. Roosevelt preferred roasted chicken. Then they were alone.

Susie could not believe she was eating dinner with Eleanor Roosevelt. How could this be happening? How could she be so lucky to be traveling with such a remarkable person to such an important meeting in Paris, France?

"I feel like pinching myself to make sure this is all really happening, but I wouldn't take the chance it is all a dream," Susie said. "This is the best birthday present any little girl could wish for," she added. And then, Susie stopped and remembered Granny Ella's gift. She looked down at her feet to make sure she still had on her red shoes. There they were, still shining and glowing…and the warmth of that glow made Susie feel like her grandmother was with her.

Just then dinner was served. As soon as Susie took her first taste, she realized how hungry she was. She tried to use her best manners and show Mrs. Roosevelt she had made the right decision to take such a grown-up young girl on this journey.

After several delicious bites, Mrs. Roosevelt asked Susie, "Is your dinner tasty? I hope you are feeling more relaxed." Just then, Susie felt a strange sensation. The sound of the propellers grew louder, and it felt like the plane was moving.

It was! As Susie looked out the small window next to her seat, she saw the plane was backing out of what she learned was called a 'hangar'. Mrs. Roosevelt's secretary came over and told Susie and Mrs. Roosevelt that they should prepare for takeoff and fasten their seat belts. Betty helped Susie snap the buckle in place.

Slowly at first, and then faster and faster, the plane raced down the paved runway; slowly at first, and then faster and faster, Susie's heart began to race. Suddenly, Susie felt a kind of pressure inside her ears, and when she looked out the window again, they were rising up and up, over the airport.

"We're flying, Mrs. Roosevelt!" Susie exclaimed.

"I know, dear child. And I am so glad you are with me on this very exciting adventure."

Susie was just as glad. After several minutes, Susie's ears felt better, and the plane no longer seemed to be climbing higher in the sky. Just then the lights in the cabin of the plane dimmed, and Susie's heart skipped a beat.

Suddenly, Susie saw a glow just as bright as her shoes, moving down the aisle. It was Mrs. Roosevelt's secretary, and she was carrying a beautiful white cake with candles. Everyone on board began singing "Happy Birthday," and a big smile filled Susie's face.

"Oh, thank you so, so much, Mrs. Roosevelt. Everything has been so amazing, I forgot it is almost my birthday."

Mrs. Roosevelt said, "I'm afraid with all the excitement tomorrow, we might not have time for a cake, Susie, so I thought we would celebrate your special birthday tonight. Now make a wish, and blow out your candles so we can all taste this yummy cake that Chef Zachary made for us."

Susie wondered how it could be her birthday when she hadn't even been born at the time Mrs. Roosevelt was alive. She decided to let well enough alone and closed her eyes to blow out the candles on her beautiful cake. She knew just what her wish would be. Quietly, so quietly that no one could hear her, Susie said to herself, "I wish that Granny Ella could see me...oh, and I also wish and hope this is not a dream."

CHAPTER EIGHT

Eleanor and Franklin

After finishing their servings of the delicious birthday cake, Mrs. Roosevelt suggested they walk back to the bedroom where Susie's suitcase was waiting. When they entered the room, Mrs. Roosevelt closed the door. The bedspreads and sheets had been pulled back on both beds, and there was a small piece of chocolate on top of each pillow.

Mrs. Roosevelt said, "I'll give you a chance to eat your bedtime treat while I get washed." It was then Susie realized that she was sharing her bedroom with the former First Lady!

When Mrs. Roosevelt came out of the bathroom, she was wearing the prettiest polka-dot nightgown and robe Susie had ever seen. Mrs. Roosevelt walked over to Susie's suitcase and took out the exact same gown and robe, only smaller. Susie could not believe her eyes.

After getting washed, Susie came out of the bathroom in her matching bedclothes and found Mrs. Roosevelt reading some papers in her bed. Susie climbed onto the other bed and asked, "Is that a bedtime story you are reading?"

Mrs. Roosevelt smiled and replied, "I am reading through my speech for tomorrow." It was then Susie remembered the importance of their journey. She imagined Mrs. Roosevelt must be even more nervous than she had been when she gave her report on the former First Lady to her class.

Mrs. Roosevelt put her papers down and said, "When my granddaughter sleeps over, once we are ready for bed, we turn off the lights and talk for a while. Would you like to do that?"

"That's just what my granny and I do when she comes to visit and sleeps in my room," Susie replied. "We talk about all kinds of things, especially what life was like for her when she was a little girl."

So Mrs. Roosevelt got up and turned off the light. "My, what a lovely red glow is filling the room, Susie," she said. "I think it is coming from your shoes. Don't you want to take them off before we fall asleep?"

"Oh, I will. But I would like to wear them just a little longer. They remind me of Granny Ella, and I miss her. Did I tell you that tomorrow is her birthday too? We were born on the same day seventy-five years apart. My granny's grandmother, Didi, gave her these shoes for her eighth birthday, and now she has given them to me. Granny Ella and I are so much alike, but we had very different childhoods."

"When I was your age, I was much more shy than you are," Mrs. Roosevelt told Susie. "Of course, things were different then. Have you ever heard the expression, 'Don't speak unless spoken to,' or 'Children should be seen and not heard'?"

Susie shook her head.

"When I was a young girl like you, Susie, children had to do exactly what their parents said, without any discussion. They did not have the opportunity to express their own thoughts and ideas. And being a young girl made it even more difficult to be heard. Did you know that for many years, women were not even allowed to vote? Those of us who spoke out on behalf of women's rights were called 'suffragettes' because we protested the way women suffered without equal rights."

"Isn't that sort of like discrimination, Mrs. Roosevelt? Not letting someone do something just because he looks different from you or has a different religion than you is a terrible thing. That's what is happening to my friend Lois and her family."

"You are correct, Susie," said Mrs. Roosevelt.

"How did you learn about all of this, Mrs. Roosevelt? Did your mother teach you about equal rights? Was your mother a suffragette?"

"No, she wasn't, Susie. By the time I was ten years old, both of my parents had died, and it wasn't until many years later that people began to think about things like equal rights. But you were right to ask about the suffragettes. They were the women who fought for fairness and equal rights for women and others who were suffering and oppressed."

"Oh, Mrs. Roosevelt, now I remember. When I was doing my school report about your life, I learned you had a very sad childhood. I am so sorry you had to live through such a terrible time."

"My family had many, many problems, Susie. My mother was a beautiful woman who was very concerned about superficial, material things and appearances. She was very involved in the sorts of social events that are attended by people who are rich and famous. Her name was Anna Livingston Hall Roosevelt, and her cousin, William Livingston, was a signer of the United States Constitution."

"That must have made life very exciting."

"I would not say those were exciting times, Susie. In fact, it was a very difficult time for my three younger brothers and me. I never felt my mother loved me; she often criticized me because I was so tall and plain looking, and I felt like I was an embarrassment to her.

"You may have read that my father, Elliot Roosevelt, was the brother of Theodore Roosevelt, the twenty-sixth president of the United States. While my father's future looked very bright, he became very sad and ill when his own mother died. He eventually had to live in a hospital.

"At the same time, my mother began to have painful headaches and became very depressed without my father at home. When I was your age, Susie, my mother died of diphtheria. All I ever wanted from her was attention and admiration. Then she was gone, and I had to accept that she would never be the kind of mother I had hoped for."

"Mrs. Roosevelt, last spring a car hit my little brother, and he could have died. It was such a scary time for him…and me. Even though growing up we sometimes had disagreements, I couldn't imagine what life would be like without him. I prayed every day that he got better… and he did.

"But it changed our whole family. I know my brother needed a lot of attention, but it was hard for me to be left out of so many things. He is almost all better now, and things are starting to get back to normal. How did you make it through such a sad time?"

"Well, Susie, to make matters worse, two years after my mother's death, my father died, and I went to live with my grandmother. Although she was very strict, I had aunts and uncles who paid attention to me, especially Uncle Theodore. When I was fifteen years old, I went to a boarding school in England."

"Oh, that must have been so terrible, Mrs. Roosevelt. I would miss my friends so much, if I went to live in another country."

"Actually Susie, I loved my school days in England. I was able to do a lot of traveling, learned several foreign languages, and made many friends. It was the first time in my life that my fears left me.

"The headmistress of the school, Mademoiselle Marie Souvestre, took a special interest in my future and taught me about the wonders of the world, as well as the troubles of people who were poor and needy. It was during this time of my life that I became interested in helping others.

"When I was seventeen, I came back to America and decided my family's rich society life was not for me. Instead, I wanted to help the poor to have a better future. So I began to work in small community centers and in the homes of little children who were living in terrible conditions.

"Two years later I met my husband, Franklin, who was actually a distant cousin of mine, and we were married. As my parents had died, it was my Uncle Theodore who walked me down the aisle on my wedding day.

"My husband was very proud of the projects I had worked on and supported the work I still wanted to do. He even helped to make it possible for me to have my own newspaper column. I wrote about the kinds of things women really needed to understand. And I even had weekly press conferences to inform all the newspapers of the progress we were making."

Susie was thrilled to hear Mrs. Roosevelt speak about the events in her life Susie had just studied. Although she missed her family, and Granny Ella in particular, being in the same room with Mrs. Roosevelt felt a lot like home.

"Well, we better get some sleep, Susie," Mrs. Roosevelt said. "Tomorrow is a big day." As they both started to drift off to sleep, the last thing Mrs. Roosevelt thought about was the warm red glow in their room. It seemed Susie had forgotten to take her shoes off after all.

CHAPTER NINE

Susie Goes to a Palace

When Susie woke up, she parted the curtain by her bed and looked out the window. To her surprise, they were no longer in the air. The plane was on the ground and rolling toward the hangar ahead of them.

At that moment, there was a soft knock on the door, and Mrs. Roosevelt's secretary asked if she could come in. Mrs. Roosevelt said, "Of course, Betty. Have we landed yet?"

"Yes, Mrs. Roosevelt. The local airport security has asked us to be prepared to leave the plane within the next hour, to make our way over to the Palais de Chaillot. We have breakfast ready for you and Susie. Oh, and there is no need to pack your things; after dinner, we will all be coming back to the plane to sleep and make our way back home."

Mrs. Roosevelt opened the suitcase she had packed for Susie and searched to find just the right outfit for their special day. She pulled out a pretty red, white, and blue jumper with a white lace blouse and blue tights.

The former First Lady held it up and said to Susie, "This will look beautiful with your wonderful red shoes."

Susie loved the outfit the minute she saw it and quickly washed, dressed, and got ready for breakfast.

As soon as they opened the door of their bedroom, Susie noticed a wonderful sweet smell coming from the dining room. "I can smell the hot chocolate. Can you, Susie?" Mrs. Roosevelt said with a smile.

Their breakfast was waiting for them. There were all sorts of coffee cakes and muffins, scrambled eggs and omelets, bacon and ham, and, of course, hot chocolate. Mrs. Roosevelt smiled at Susie and said, "Happy birthday, sweetheart. This is the first meal of the first day of the eighth year of your life." And with that, she leaned over and gave Susie a gentle kiss on her forehead.

After the plane had pulled into the hangar, the former First Lady's staff helped Mrs. Roosevelt and Susie toward the door and down the steps. An amazingly huge and beautiful silver car was waiting to take them to their destination. "They have sent a very elegant Rolls-Royce for us, Susie. Maybe that's a sign that the delegates are happy we have arrived."

As their car drove through Paris, Mrs. Roosevelt pointed out the window at many beautiful sights she had obviously seen before. "There is the Arc de Triomphe, Susie, and over there is the River Seine, my dear. If you look on the right side of the river, you will see a very big hill called Chaillot Hill. And the huge building that sits on the top of Chaillot Hill is the Palais de Chaillot. That is where we are going for our meeting."

Their car pulled up in front of the most gorgeous building Susie had ever seen. Brilliant gold statues glistened in the sunshine. There were two main buildings connected by a beautiful terrace that overlooked the river.

As soon as the door of the car was opened, it seemed like the Fourth of July. There were so many cameras and flash bulbs going off that at first, it was hard for Susie to see the beauty of the palace.

Once she stepped outside, the photographers were shouting at Mrs. Roosevelt to look their way. When Susie appeared, they called out, "Please, Mrs. Roosevelt. Who is the young girl with you?"

Mrs. Roosevelt smiled as she looked at Susie and reached for her hand. "She is my very special, brave friend and a human-rights leader in her community. She has come on this journey with me so children all over the world can see they too have the opportunity to make a difference."

Susie thought her heart would burst with pride. She knew she would not disappoint the former First Lady. And while Susie still did not know exactly what she would or could do to help her friend back home, she had faith the answers would soon come to her.

CHAPTER TEN

Nations United

As they walked down the long, marble hallway, Susie didn't know what to look at first. There were enormous crystal chandeliers that cast shadows of rainbows across the floor. Gold-framed portraits of kings and queens lined the walls. The carpets seemed to stretch for miles and miles, as did the row of people who were lined up to meet and greet the former First Lady and her guest.

"What made you decide to come to this meeting, Mrs. Roosevelt?" Susie asked. "Was this meeting your idea?"

"Oh, no. I can't take credit for that. In 1945, the year my dear Franklin died, President Truman appointed me to be a delegate to the first meeting of the General Assembly of the United Nations. That meeting was held in London, England, right after World War II.

"During the war, so many people in so many countries were hurt and saddened. They felt alone and afraid because of all the damage that had been done. Before he died, my husband, Franklin, and other leaders of the countries who fought alongside America, felt the future would be safer and brighter if the nations of the world united and worked together.

"The United Nations got its name in 1942, when twenty-six nations signed a declaration. They pledged to support each other, united, as if they were one nation. Their goal was to find a way to win the war and help each other solve problems without having to fight in the future. At that first meeting of the UN, I was asked to be the chairman of the Commission on Human Rights. Our job was to write an International Bill of Rights, like the Bill of Rights that was written for America's own constitution many years ago.

"Today, I will be presenting the ideas our commission decided could make the world a better place. And if things go well, the delegates at this meeting of the United Nations will accept what we are recommending. It's like what we do in America when congressmen write bills that then get passed by the House of Representatives and the Senate. Instead of representatives from our forty-eight states, delegates from the more than fifty nations who belong to the United Nations are the ones who will hopefully embrace our International Bill of Rights."

After what seemed like a two-mile walk, Mrs. Roosevelt and Susie approached two carved doors that looked like they were made of gold. As Susie stared up at them, a very dignified man with a very French accent said, "These doors are made of solid bronze and the pictures carved on them tell the history of the French empire." Then two other very serious-looking men wearing what looked like military uniforms, each held one of the handles and opened the enormous doors.

What they saw before them was so grand, Susie could hardly breathe. Hanging from a ceiling that seemed to reach the sky were three spectacular, glittering chandeliers, suspended from what looked like chains of gold. The ceiling itself was covered with golden branches, leaves, and flowers. The walls surrounding the room were decorated with carved pillars and between every two pillars was a flag from a different nation.

At the front of the room was a stage with blue velvet curtains that reached the ceiling. The edges were gold fringed and gold *fleur de lis* had been embroidered on the valence hanging from above. A long table spanned the stage, covered with the same blue velvet. Behind the table, raised on a platform, were two tall, carved, golden chairs fit for a king and queen. In front of the table was a speaker's platform where Susie guessed Mrs. Roosevelt would stand to give her speech.

Most of the seats in the room were already filled, and most of the people were speaking in languages Susie could not understand. As she and Mrs. Roosevelt were led toward the front of the room, the former First Lady stopped along the way, greeting people she must have met before.

Many of the people who reached out to Mrs. Roosevelt did not speak English. Susie was amazed that the former First Lady was able to understand what each person was saying and converse with him in his own language. Then Susie remembered that Mrs. Roosevelt had gone to boarding school in England and had studied foreign languages.

When they reached the front of the room, there were several empty seats. Mrs. Roosevelt took Susie's hand as they were led to the very front row. When she turned around to look at all the people sitting behind her, Susie Gardner, from Merion, Pennsylvania, knew she was a witness to one of the most important moments in the history of the world.

CHAPTER ELEVEN

A Standing Ovation

Before she was called to the stage, Mrs. Roosevelt spoke quietly to Susie. "You know, my dear, up to now the way a country treated its people was thought to be that country's own business. But when the world saw what happened during this last war, we realized that all of us have the right and responsibility to watch over each and every person…to fight for the human rights of all human beings."

After the dignitaries took their seats on the stage, Mrs. Roosevelt was introduced to the General Assembly. Every man, woman, and one child stood up and applauded her for her courage and determination. As the former First Lady approached the podium, the man sitting behind Susie tapped her on the shoulder and said, "You know, my dear child, Mrs. Roosevelt is not only a First Lady of your country; she is the First Lady of the world!" Susie was so proud to be in the presence of such an inspiring woman.

Mrs. Roosevelt began by telling the audience how long and hard her committee had worked to write the Declaration of Human Rights. She explained that the most important thing to understand and remember was that all people were entitled to equal protection and that no man should be forced to be a servant to another man. She spoke about freedom and the things that make people civilized and human. She asked the members to agree to this declaration and give all people the dignity they deserved.

As the First Lady of the world continued presenting the ideas of her committee, Susie was reminded of what had happened to her friend's family back in Merion, Pennsylvania. It just did not seem possible, considering all the things being discussed at this meeting, that the people in her own town would think of denying others their human rights, just because of their religion.

In the end, Mrs. Roosevelt asked the assembly,

> Let this third regular session of the General Assembly approve by an overwhelming majority the Declaration of Human Rights as a standard of conduct for all; and let us, as Members of the United Nations, conscious of our own shortcomings and imperfections, join our effort in good faith to live up to this high standard.

When the former First Lady finished her speech, there was thunderous applause. The delegates were all standing and continued to clap and cheer for more than five minutes. Mrs. Roosevelt stood tall and proud as she looked out at all the people in the room. When she looked down at Susie and winked at her young friend, Susie smiled and waved to Mrs. Roosevelt.

As she left the stage and made her way back to her seat, delegates rushed to congratulate her. Everyone was moving toward the front of the room, and for a moment, Susie lost sight of Mrs. Roosevelt.

Suddenly, Susie felt an arm around her shoulders. She looked up to see Mrs. Roosevelt looking down at her with a big smile on her face. "So Susie, do you think they will accept our Bill of Rights?"

"Oh, yes, Mrs. Roosevelt. You were amazing and this is the most amazing day of my life. Everyone is so excited. They all love you! Who wouldn't agree with this declaration?" As soon as she said those words, Susie thought about the Wynnehall Country Club.

Just then, an announcement was made for the members of the assembly to head toward the grand ballroom for lunch and further discussions. Susie and Mrs. Roosevelt were led to a side door so they would not have to make their way through the crowd of very excited delegates.

Through a long, winding, narrow marble hall, and then down a wide, circular staircase, the two women were escorted to what felt like a secret hiding place. At the bottom of the stairs was a small brass door. It was not nearly as fancy as the one to the auditorium and had a very large lock and keyhole.

One of the distinguished gentlemen who had led them to the door took out one of the largest keys Susie had ever seen. It was so heavy he had to use two hands to place it in the keyhole and turn it.

When the door opened, the sight of the grand ballroom took Susie by surprise. Even Mrs. Roosevelt was stunned by the beauty and elegance of the room.

All of the walls were mirrored, and because the ceiling was painted pale blue, it seemed to reach to the sky. There were gold trimmings everywhere, and the crystal chandeliers were even bigger than those hanging in the hallways and auditorium. The ballroom was filled with large round tables, all of which were covered with layers of lace tablecloths. The light from the chandeliers shone down on the crystal glassware, china dishes, and silverware in a way that made the whole room sparkle.

At the front of the ballroom was a buffet table filled with every wonderful dish Susie could imagine. There were whole roasted chickens, whole roasted fish, shrimp, and lobsters. There were roasted potatoes, mashed potatoes, and even French fries. Salads and platters piled high with fruits and vegetables were also prepared for the delegates. And then Susie saw the desserts.

Among all the pies, cookies, ice creams, and cakes, one special dessert caught her eye. On a gold cake stand was a chocolate cake that looked dark and rich and somewhat familiar to Susie. It was not as fancy as the other cakes; it had no icing and was just sprinkled with powdered sugar. As she looked at it, Susie could almost taste it.

Slowly, the delegates began to enter the room. They were encouraged to walk past the buffet and then take their seats. Susie and Mrs. Roosevelt were seated with the American and French delegates. Each table had a butler and three servers who asked each person what he or she preferred to eat and then brought back a plate from the buffet table.

Even though Mrs. Roosevelt spoke perfect French, as soon as the conversation at their table began, the former First Lady politely asked the French delegates to speak in English. "I want my young friend to hear your thoughts and understand your points of view so that she can teach her friends back in America how to discuss their differences and find solutions that work for everyone."

From what Susie heard, it seemed the members were worried the Russian delegates might not agree to the declaration. As each person made suggestions,

Mrs. Roosevelt listened patiently. After they all had had a chance to voice their concerns, the former First Lady began to speak. Susie noticed how carefully everyone listened to Mrs. Roosevelt, nodding and smiling as they felt her sincerity and passion; they seemed to agree with her and became less anxious and more hopeful.

CHAPTER TWELVE

What Does 'Gooey' Mean?

When everyone finished eating lunch, the servers cleared the table and began to prepare for dessert. When Susie was asked what she would like from the buffet, she said, "I can't wait to try that chewy, gooey, dark chocolate fudge cake."

Everyone looked at her, and one of the French delegates asked, "What is 'gooey,' young lady?" But the butler seemed to understand just what Susie was talking about.

When Susie's dessert plate arrived, she took her fork and gave the Frenchman a taste. "Now do you understand?" Susie said.

He smiled and nodded. "Yes, I understand 'gooey' and 'chewy,' *mademoiselle*." Everyone at the table, including Mrs. Roosevelt, laughed.

The cake was just as delicious as Susie remembered… or thought she remembered. But where could she have tasted it before? This was her first and only trip to Paris. When the servers asked if anyone wanted anything else.

Susie smiled and, using a little of the French she had overheard during the past few hours, said, "*S'il vous plaît, monsieur.* Could I have another piece of the chocolate cake?" Everyone at the table smiled, and Mrs. Roosevelt gave Susie a little hug of approval. Then three other delegates also asked for another piece of the chewy, gooey, dark chocolate fudge cake.

When the butler came to take the orders for tea and coffee, Mrs. Roosevelt motioned for him to bend down so she could whisper something in his ear. He smiled, and as he walked away, he said, "I will bring that to you shortly, *madame.*" Ten minutes later, he came back to the table with an envelope. He leaned down and said to Susie, "*Pour vous, mademoiselle.*"

Susie could not imagine what was inside. Who would write her a letter? Who even knew she was in Paris, France? Mrs. Roosevelt watched as Susie opened the envelope and then heard her young friend laugh out loud.

"What is it, my dear?" the former First Lady asked.

But Susie had a feeling Mrs. Roosevelt already knew. "It's the recipe for the chewy, gooey, dark chocolate fudge cake!" Susie answered. "I will take this home to America with me and make it for my family. Granny Ella will just love it, and she won't believe where it came from." And right then, Susie realized there was truth to what she just said. Her grandmother really might not believe her when she told her where she had been.

Just then, the butler asked Susie if she would like to come back to the kitchen to take a quick tour and meet the chef who prepared the chocolate cake. Susie looked over at Mrs. Roosevelt to see what she thought of the idea.

Mrs. Roosevelt said, "I suppose that could be very interesting, my dear. Betty, would you go along to make sure Susie finds her way there and back again?"

"I would be pleased to do so, Mrs. Roosevelt," Betty replied as she and Susie got up from the table. The butler led them back past the buffet table and then through the small brass door where they had entered the ballroom. Instead of going up the spiral staircase, they turned right and made their way down a long hall. Servers were rushing back and forth with trays, and it appeared the kitchen was straight ahead.

Then the butler showed Susie and Betty into what seemed to be a small storage room. He told them Chef Chevronelle would be right there to greet them and begin their tour. However, as he left the room and closed the door, Susie thought she heard the door lock.

When Susie looked over at Betty, she saw the older woman had a concerned look on her face. Betty walked over to the door to try the knob and found that it would not turn. They were locked in!

Betty saw a phone on the desk and went over to call for help, but there was no dial tone. When she looked at the cord, she saw it had been pulled from the wall. Betty turned to Susie and said, "Do not worry, my dear. We will figure out what is going on and be back with Mrs. Roosevelt before you know it."

CHAPTER THIRTEEN

A Light in the Dark

Susie was worried. Betty put on a brave face and assured her that with all the important delegates at the palace for the meeting of the UN Assembly, no harm would come to them. Someone would notice they were missing and come looking for them shortly. But Susie could tell Betty was just as worried as she was.

"The last time I was this scared was when a car hit my brother, Bennett, last spring," Susie told Betty. "I knew he needed me to be strong and confident, or he would have been even more upset."

"That was a very wise approach, Susie. We are two smart women; if we think this through, I am sure we can come up with a plan."

"Last night on the plane, Mrs. Roosevelt told me about the difficult times she had growing up. By conquering her fears and being brave, she has accomplished so many wonderful things. She is my role model, and we must try to be as strong as she is," Susie said.

"I agree," said Betty. "When I was about your age, my younger sister and I shared a bedroom. One night we were sound asleep when her coughing woke me up. As

I sat up in bed, I could not see her because smoke had completely filled the room. I knew this meant our house was on fire. I called out to my sister and told her I would come and get her.

"In school, we had learned what to do in case of a fire, and I knew I had to remain calm. I got down on the floor, crawled into our bathroom, and wet two washcloths. Then I crawled back to my sister and got her out of bed. We held the damp towels over our eyes, noses, and mouths and crawled over to the bedroom window.

"When I reached my desk, I grabbed a paperweight and threw it at the window. Cool air filled the room. When I looked out, I saw a fire truck speeding down the road. I waved my washcloth out the window, and before we knew it, a fireman came up a ladder and rescued us.

"So you are right, Susie. Staying calm is what saved my life and my sister's, and it can help us now. Oh, and you won't be surprised to know Mrs. Roosevelt is my role model, too."

The story about Betty and the fire reminded Susie of something. They moved closer to the door and tried to listen for someone passing by. But the walls of the palace were so thick that Susie and Betty doubted they could hear much of anything or that anyone could hear them if they called out for help.

Then Susie noticed that there was a gap between the heavy wooden door and the stone floor. She could see light shining through. Suddenly that light was disrupted, and it appeared someone was standing in the hallway by the door. Susie got down on the floor to listen, to see if it were someone who could help them. What she heard next was shocking.

"Why did you not bring Mrs. Roosevelt, too? That was the plan, you fool. What good will taking the secretary and a little girl do?"

The other man replied, "Do not worry. The meeting will not proceed as long as these friends of Mrs. Roosevelt are missing. While they search for them, the discussion will be delayed."

"We must move them to a safer hiding place, more out of the way," the first man said. "When we open the door, quickly move them away from the kitchen area and down to the basement. Tell them the chef will be meeting them in the pantry area."

Susie realized they had to think of a plan—and quickly, too. The future of the declaration was at stake. She knew that if they left the office they could be in even worse trouble. Betty told Susie that she had an idea.

When the door opened, Betty was lying on the floor. The butler rushed over to her, and in a very weak voice Betty said, "Please help me. I am very sick! I think it is my heart. My medicine is in my purse at our table in the ballroom. You must get it for me." And then Betty's eyes closed, and it appeared to Susie and the butler she had passed out.

The butler told Susie, "Unless you want your friend to die, you will be very quiet." He took several dinner napkins and tied Susie's hands and ankles. He then used another napkin as a gag to keep Susie from calling for help. He then tied Susie to a chair with cooking twine and rushed out the door. Once again, Susie heard the sound of the door locking.

As Susie looked down at Betty, she was so afraid... until Betty opened her eyes and winked at her. Betty got up and pulled the gag down from Susie's mouth and untied her. She told Susie, "If they go back to our table and tell Mrs. Roosevelt I need the medicine in my purse, Mrs. Roosevelt will be very suspicious. I have no medicine in my purse, and Mrs. Roosevelt knows that. Just you wait and see, Susie. She will find us."

That was just what the butler was afraid of too. He knew that if Mrs. Roosevelt heard her secretary was ill, she would be suspicious. She and the other delegates at her table would want to get to the woman and child as quickly as possible. However, if the secretary really was ill, he did not want the woman to die. He had to find another way.

Susie also knew she had to find a way for Betty and her to be rescued and make sure the declaration succeeded. She noticed light was still coming in under the door. This reminded her of her brother, Bennett, and the night Granny Ella gave Susie her new shoes. When Susie thought about the story Betty told her of the fire in her house, Susie had an idea and quietly told Betty to turn off the light in the room.

Although she did not know why her young friend wanted her to do this, Betty got up and flipped off the wall switch. At first, the room was dark. But that was soon to change.

CHAPTER FOURTEEN

The Butler Did It!

The butler had a plan. He would have to steal the purse. And he could not let his accomplice know there had been a setback. So he went back into the kitchen, took one of the large serving trays, covered it with a large serving cloth, and headed back to the ballroom.

When the butler approached Mrs. Roosevelt's table, she asked him how the tour of the kitchen was progressing. "Oh, the chef is giving them the royal treatment, Mrs. Roosevelt. By the time I clear these last few things from the table, your friends will be returning to the ballroom."

He saw the strap from the pocketbook hanging on the back of the secretary's chair. In a quick move, the butler dropped a fork on the floor. When he bent down to pick it up, he removed the strap from the chair and tried to pull the purse onto the tray and cover it with the serving cloth. But it seemed to be caught on something.

As the butler pulled harder on the strap, Mrs. Roosevelt stood up, holding the purse in her hands. "What do you think you are doing?" she shouted. "Are you trying to steal from us?"

The French delegates jumped to their feet. They grabbed the butler, pushed him down on the floor, and held him there until help arrived.

"Where are my friends, young man? Tell us right now, or you will be in more trouble than you can imagine," Mrs. Roosevelt said.

"We want you to stop the discussion of the declaration. If the delegates leave the Palais de Chaillot, we will let them go," the butler replied.

Just then, the president of the UN Assembly arrived at the table, looked at the butler, and said, "Vladimir, what are you doing? How did you get into the Palais de Chaillot?"

He turned to the French officers who were approaching and said, "Arrest this man. He is in this country illegally. We have been looking for him and his brother, Grigori, for the past month. They have vowed to disrupt our meeting to prevent the acceptance of the Declaration of Human Rights."

"And we have succeeded! You will never see your friends again unless all the delegates leave the ballroom at once! No declaration can tell us what we can and cannot do in our own land."

A moment later, Mrs. Roosevelt heard someone calling her name. It was Susie! And Betty was right behind her. The butler looked at the pair with disbelief. And then he saw his brother being led to the table…in handcuffs!

As Mrs. Roosevelt rushed over to hug her two friends, she said, "Susie! Betty! I am so happy to see you. Are you all right? How did you get away from these two scoundrels?"

Betty looked over at Susie and smiled. "You won't believe it, Mrs. Roosevelt. They left us in an abandoned storage room. I told them I needed some of my heart medicine and then pretended to pass out. They tied Susie up and left us alone to get what they thought was in my purse. When I took the gag out from Susie's mouth, she told me to turn off the light. And suddenly, there in the dark, a brilliant red glow filled the room. I don't know where it came from."

Susie continued. "Before we knew it, Mrs. Roosevelt, officers were breaking down the door. The men also saw the red glow coming from under the door where we were being held, thought there was a fire, and they rescued us!"

The officer in charge turned to Mrs. Roosevelt and said, "How did you capture this one?"

Mrs. Roosevelt replied, "When Betty left with Susie for their tour of the palace kitchen, I noticed she forgot her pocketbook. Rather than just leave it hanging by the strap on her chair, I held the bag on my lap until Betty and Susie returned. When Vladimir came back to our table, and I felt someone tugging on the pocketbook, I suspected he was trying to steal it."

Then Mrs. Roosevelt turned and glared at the brothers, both of whom were now in handcuffs. Before they were led away, she wanted to try to make them understand what the declaration was really about. "In giving our approval to this declaration today, we are all aware that it is not a treaty or a statement of law. It is a statement of basic principles of human rights and freedoms. It will help lift men everywhere to a higher standard of life and to a greater enjoyment of life.

"This declaration is a moral standard of conduct for us all. While we will not agree on every issue and point, it challenges every one of us to make a good faith effort to live up to that higher standard. You have nothing to fear from this document.

"It will, when accepted, help you and the people you love and care about to have a better life. It will hopefully help all people find the peace and dignity you want for yourselves, your loved ones, and your country. And this declaration will set standards that will make certain you are both treated humanely during what will probably be a very long stay in prison."

CHAPTER FIFTEEN

A Picture is Worth a Thousand Words

As the brothers were taken away, one of the two distinguished men who had led the Roosevelt party to the ballroom approached Betty. Mrs. Roosevelt's secretary leaned over and quietly whispered to Mrs. Roosevelt, "I have just been informed the car is waiting to take us back to the plane. We should probably be on our way to the airport."

After they said their good-byes and began walking along the cool, dim hallways, Betty noticed the same red glow that had filled the storage room earlier. She tried to see where the light was coming from. Eventually, her eyes drifted down to the floor. Susie's shoes were glowing! When Betty put her arm around Susie's shoulder, their eyes met, and they smiled.

To Susie's surprise, there were still hundreds of people waiting outside to see the delegates one last time. As she looked down the steps and out into the crowd, Susie suddenly noticed a woman who looked familiar.

She had very curly blond hair and a big smile with bright red lipstick, and she was waving an American flag at the American delegation.

As Susie watched this woman, a special warm feeling rushed through her heart. Susie saw she was talking with a group of other women who looked like her friends. Just then someone took a picture of the little group with the woman's camera.

There was something familiar and special about the woman. Susie reached into her pocket and took out the envelope with the recipe for the chocolate cake. Susie looked at it more carefully than she had inside the palace and was shocked when she read the name of the cake. Although she had thought it would have some fancy French name, Susie was quite surprised to see it was called "Granny's chewy, gooey, dark chocolate fudge cake."

CHAPTER SIXTEEN

Au Revoir, Paris!

The next thing Susie knew, she was back in the silver car with Mrs. Roosevelt. Her head was spinning from all she had seen and been through that day. Suddenly, she was missing her family and was excited at the thought of telling them all about her adventure. But what would they think? Would they believe what seemed impossible?

The sun was setting, and they were seeing their last glimpses of Paris as the car headed back to the airport. The city was all aglow, and every light in every building and every light on every bridge that crossed the Seine electrified the evening sky. Mrs. Roosevelt turned to Susie and said, "This is why Paris is known as the 'City of Lights'!"

As they boarded the presidential plane, Mrs. Roosevelt suggested they get washed and ready for bed. They would sleep on the plane and be back on American soil when they awoke the next day.

Susie's feet were tired from all the walking they had done. But her shoes had not lost their sparkle nor their glow. And when Susie climbed into the bed next to Mrs.

Roosevelt's, she decided to leave her shoes on for just a little while longer.

Susie looked over at the former First Lady and said, "Aren't you proud of what happened today, Mrs. Roosevelt?"

Her new friend smiled at her and said, "Yes, Susie, I am. But I am also proud that you came with me and were a witness to history being made."

Mrs. Roosevelt paused and then said, "Susie, I believe these countries will now try to make the world a better and safer place, but I also believe it will take people like you, one person at a time, who will stand up for justice and equality, to really make a difference. I asked you before we arrived in Paris if you thought you were brave enough to make a difference in the world. What do you think?"

Susie smiled and said, "Oh, Mrs. Roosevelt, I know I am!" Susie was proud of herself for trusting her instincts and coming on this trip. She was also proud that, even though she did not really understand how all of this was possible, she was brave enough to give it a try. She was especially proud of the way she and Betty had stayed calm and brave when they were kidnapped and figured out a way to be rescued.

Mrs. Roosevelt smiled at her and said, "The meeting went as well as it could have. And now, the destiny of human rights is in the hands of all the delegates and the citizens in all the communities of the world."

The warm red glow that filled the room reminded Susie that she was still wearing her red birthday shoes. She couldn't wait to tell Granny Ella about Mrs. Roosevelt, the plane, Paris, and the ballroom. And she couldn't wait to bake the chewy, gooey, dark chocolate fudge cake for her grandmother. Susie reached down, took off her shoes, and placed them on the floor next to her bed. She could still see the lights of Paris as she watched the plane climb higher and higher in the sky. Before Susie knew it, she was fast asleep.

CHAPTER SEVENTEEN

Happy Birthday!

Susie woke up to the sound of gentle tapping on the bedroom door. "Wake up, you two sleepyheads. It's your birthday, and there are lots of presents down here for you to unwrap."

Susie rolled over, expecting to see the former First Lady waking from her sleep. "Oh, I slept so well, Mrs. Roosevelt." But instead of seeing Mrs. Roosevelt in the bed next to hers, Susie's Granny Ella looked over at her with a surprised look on her face.

"What did you just call me, sweetheart?" her grandmother said. "You must have been having a dream about your school report. It sounded like you called me 'Mrs. Roosevelt'!"

Susie sat up in bed, feeling confused. Where had Mrs. Roosevelt gone? How did Granny Ella get into their bedroom on the plane? Then Susie realized she was back in her own room. The next thing she knew, her mother was coming through the door.

"Happy birthday, Susie and Mom!" her mother said. "How late did you two stay up talking? It's ten in the morning, and the whole family is waiting downstairs for you. Get dressed, and come down to see what we have for you."

Susie got out of bed and slipped on her new red shoes. When Granny Ella saw her granddaughter do this, she said, "Oh, Susie. You must really love my special birthday present. That makes me so happy."

Susie said, "They are my most special thing in the whole world, Granny." Susie wanted to tell her grandmother how much Mrs. Roosevelt loved the shoes too, but it didn't feel like the right time to do so. So she put on her jeans and favorite T-shirt and waited for Granny Ella to get dressed. Then they both went downstairs to be greeted with birthday cheers from their family.

"Look at Susie's shoesies," her brother, Bennett, said. Everyone laughed. On the dining room table were platters of pancakes, scrambled eggs, bacon, and home-fried potatoes. There were all kinds of jellies, pancake syrups, and hot chocolate too. Susie was excited to begin the first meal of her birthday. Or was it? Didn't she have a birthday breakfast with Mrs. Roosevelt on the plane? Was it still 1948, or was Susie back to the year 2007?

After breakfast, everyone gathered in the living room as Susie's father brought in presents for her and Granny Ella. They took turns opening them.

Bennett had gotten Susie a package of twenty-four pencils with her name on them. Susie laughed and gave her brother a knowing smile. This was the perfect gift for his big sister. In the past, whenever he was looking for something to write with, he would sneak into Susie's room and take a pencil from her desk. Then, when Susie would start to do her homework, she couldn't find anything with which to write.

Bennett had picked out a pair of gardening gloves for his grandmother. "Now the thorns on our rose bushes won't prick your hands any more," he said. Granny Ella gave him a big hug and kiss.

Susie could not believe her eyes when she saw what her mother and father had gotten her—her very own laptop computer! Now she and Bennett would not argue over who got to use the family computer. Susie knew the first thing she would use her new gift for was to research the 1948 meeting of the General Assembly of the United Nations and the Universal Declaration of Human Rights. And when she did so, Susie wondered if there would be any mention of the attempt to disrupt the meeting.

Her parents then handed Granny Ella an envelope and said, "Happy birthday, Mom." When she opened the card that was inside, Granny Ella saw two airline tickets… to Paris, France!

Granny Ella started to cry tears of joy as she hugged each member of her family. "I have always wanted to go back to Paris. It has been so many, many years since I was there."

Susie's mom said, "You can pick whomever you want to go with you. This will be a very special trip for a very special lady and some very special friend."

Granny Ella looked over at Susie and gave her a subtle wink. Susie laughed but was not quite sure what this sign meant. Did her granny know where Susie had been? Susie wondered whether she really had been anywhere besides her own bedroom or was her grandmother thinking of taking Susie with her to Paris?

Next came a big box for Susie from her Aunt Merry and Uncle Dave. It was a new bathing suit, matching robe, and flip-flops. She would wear it to Irene Baron's birthday party at the country club, Susie thought to herself. It was then she remembered what was going on. Would Irene really switch her party to another club rather than go back to the one that treated the Bernsteins so badly?

Susie opened several other lovely gifts from aunts and cousins. One of her presents was a book about a woman named Wilma Rudolph. The card inside said,

> *Susie, you will enjoy reading about this amazing woman who had just as much spunk and determination as you do. Your mom told us you have read a lot about the Roosevelts. As you read about Wilma Rudolph, you will see what she has in common with them.*
>
> *With love, Aunt Linda and Uncle Bill*

Finally, there was one last gift to be opened. As she carefully unwrapped the package and opened the box, Susie saw the most amazing thing inside. It was the polka-dot nightgown and robe she remembered wearing on the plane to Paris, the one that matched Mrs. Roosevelt's.

There was no card inside to say who had sent the gift, however, Susie knew it could only be from one person. But how could that be?

Susie looked at Granny Ella, who smiled and said, "What a beautiful gift, Susie. Who is it from?"

Susie said, "Oh, one of my really special friends sent this to me."

CHAPTER EIGHTEEN

More Trouble at the Country Club

Once the breakfast dishes were cleaned up and all the boxes and wrapping paper were put away, Susie remembered the chocolate cake recipe she was given in Paris. She wanted to give it to Granny Ella as a going-home present. Susie rushed up to her bedroom and searched through all her pockets and in all her drawers, but the envelope was nowhere to be found.

Susie came back downstairs and looked for her mother. She had a hunch. "Mom, where is your recipe for the chewy, gooey, dark chocolate fudge cake?" Her mother went over to the shelf above the stove, where she kept all of her cookbooks and recipes, and pulled down her recipe box. She quickly took out an index card and handed it to Susie.

To her daughter's surprise, the recipe looked very old and worn. But it was the name of the cake that surprised Susie the most. It was called "Granny's chewy, gooey, dark chocolate fudge cake." The writing looked just like the writing Susie remembered on her copy of the recipe she was given in Paris.

Susie's mother had been watching her daughter and noticed she looked confused. "What's the matter, dear?" her mother asked.

Susie looked up and said, "Mom, where did this recipe come from? Who gave it to you?"

Just then, Granny Ella came into the kitchen and said, "I found that recipe on the street in Paris, France, during that trip I told you about, Susie. I guess someone invented the cake for his or her grandmother. When I got home, I followed the recipe and found it made the wonderful cake we all love. As I do not do much baking any more, I passed the recipe down to your mother."

Now Susie was really confused. She was sure it was the exact copy of the recipe she got at the Palais de Chaillot. Susie wondered if this was the right time to tell her mother and grandmother about her amazing adventure. But at this point, Susie did not know what had really happened. She asked herself, "Did I really go to Paris…or did I dream it?"

Susie's dad came into the kitchen and announced that he had an idea. "Let's help Granny Ella pack up and take her out for lunch on our way to the airport."

Bennett heard the plan and said, "Good thinkin', Mr. Blinkin."

Susie and her grandmother went upstairs and, in about an hour, came back down with Granny Ella's suitcase. The family got into the SUV and off they went for their favorite lunch treat. They arrived at Pat's Cheesesteaks and after parking the car, made their way around the corner to order their food.

There, Susie was surprised to see her friend Irene Baron and her family in line ahead of them. Susie's dad was very good friends with Peter Baron and went over to him and said, "Hey Pete! Why aren't you at the board of directors' meeting at the club?"

Mr. Baron replied, "Well, Eric. I won't be serving on the board any longer. Actually, we are not going back to the club at all. Did you hear what happened when the Bernsteins applied for membership?"

Eric Gardner knew just what his friend was referring to. "Yes, Susie was telling us about it. Is it true they were not allowed to join Wynnehall and were told to join another club...because they were Jewish?"

"It seems so," Peter Baron said. "When Irene told me what the girls were talking about at school, I went to see Mr. Gage, the club manager, myself. I was absolutely shocked when he told me, 'The Bernsteins will be happier at a club with their own kind of people.'

"I told him, 'Well, we are their kind of people, so maybe we don't belong at Wynnehall either!' When I turned to walk away, he didn't even apologize or try to stop me. Gail and I have already written our letter of resignation, and we have applied to join the Overhill Country Club, along with Eli and Danit Bernstein. I also called Larry and Sally Taylor, Brynne Carson, and Ross Harrison, They are also resigning from Wynnehall and making an application to join Overhill."

As the two families sat together and ate lunch, they continued to discuss the situation. Granny Ella looked over at Susie and said, "You know something about this, don't you, sweetheart?"

Susie told the group about her research on Eleanor Roosevelt and said, "We have to do more than just walk away. We have to let everyone know that Wynnehall Country Club discriminates. Why don't we picket in front of the club next Saturday evening? That's when they are holding the celebrity auction and dinner dance. Reporters will be there to cover the event, and they might be very interested in what's going on."

Susie's granny had some advice. "I think that as long as you stay on the sidewalk and do not block the driveway or entrance, they will have to allow you to picket. But you should go to the town hall and check with the supervisors, just to be sure you won't be breaking any laws."

Susie thought for a minute and said, "We will make signs and bring candles with us too. Mrs. Roosevelt said, 'It is better to light a candle than to curse the darkness.'" Susie turned to her friend Irene and said, "After we get home from taking my granny to the airport, I will call you, Jaden, Samantha, Becky, and Rachel to come over and help us plan our protest. What do you think?"

"Susie, I think you and Mrs. Roosevelt are right. This is an important thing to do. But I'm a little afraid we might get into trouble."

To that, Susie replied, "Remember what President Franklin Roosevelt said? 'The only thing we have to fear is fear itself.'"

The Gardners left the restaurant and headed to the airport. It was time for Granny Ella to fly home to Greensburg. Susie was sad to see her go, especially because she did not know when she would see her grandmother again. But then she had an idea. "Granny Ella, you might be able to see me next Sunday, if we make the news. I will call you and let you know what happened."

Her grandmother put her arms around Susie and said, "I am so proud of you, sweetheart. You really are a very brave young girl."

Without thinking, Susie said, "That's what Mrs. Roosevelt said, too."

Her grandmother thought she must have not been listening carefully to what Susie had said and replied,

"You are right, Susie. Mrs. Roosevelt would think you were very brave, and she would be just as proud of you as we are."

When they arrived at the airport, everyone got out to kiss and hug Granny Ella good-bye. Bennett was so upset to see her go that he was crying. Susie put her arm around him and said, "Come on now. She will be back again soon. And Bennett, we have a lot to do this week to get ready for our protest. This will be a week to remember."

CHAPTER NINETEEN

Guess Who's on the Six O'Clock News?

A week later, just a little before six o'clock in the evening, Susie picked up the phone and dialed her grandmother's number in Greensburg. On the second ring, she heard her granny's voice.

"Granny Ella, you are not going to believe what has happened! You have to turn on channel three. We are going to be on the news!"

"Susie, tell me what's going on," said Granny Ella.

Susie could hear that her grandmother was just as excited as she was. "Well, just like we said we were going to do, all week long, my friends and Bennett and I made posters. It was Bennett's idea to have the words rhyme. Our signs said, 'If they can't stay, we'll all walk away!' We found out we had to get a permit to have a peaceful protest, so Mom took me to town hall, and they showed me how to fill out the proper papers.

"Granny, it was so exciting. They had two policemen come to keep everyone safe. They helped us and showed us where to march and where we were not allowed to go. It was just like you thought. There were rules we had to follow, like being careful not to block the entrance to the club.

"But guess what happened? When Chef Brown and the waiters arrived at the club to set up for the silent auction, they would not cross our picket line. Without them, there was no one to make the food or serve it to the members. When the auction was over, most of the guests left Wynnehall. And guess where they all went for dinner? To the Overhill Country Club!

"And Granny, the TV cameras filmed the whole thing. They interviewed all of us, and we told them how terrible we thought it was that the Bernsteins were not allowed to join Wynnehall. The newspaper took pictures of us too and said that we would make the front page of the morning paper. I can't believe it!

"My dad said that in the middle of all the commotion, he saw the president of the board of the country club drive in; five minutes later, Mr. Gage, the manager, drove out looking very upset. Then Stanley Howard, the golf pro, came out and spoke to Dad and told him Mr. Gage was fired!"

Granny Ella was so proud of her granddaughter. "You are quite an amazing young girl, Susie. You have done a very important thing, standing up for your friend. And even more importantly, you have changed the way that country club, and maybe all country clubs, will treat people in the future."

Then Bennett got on the phone and said, "Oh, Ella Bella…you should have been here. It was so exciting. The reporter said that Susie was a hero! My sister is a hero!"

Susie told her brother that she was especially proud of him. "Bennett, you were the youngest protester there. And without your slogan, we would not have been as successful. I am very proud of you."

"Merion, Pennsylvania, will never be quite the same," Granny Ella said. "I'm going to go turn on the TV so I don't miss the news. I'll call you later tonight."

Just then, Susie's mom called out, "It's on right now. Come here, all of you, right away. Susie and Bennett are on TV! Oh my goodness. All the kids are there. Everyone is there!"

For the next three minutes, the reporter told the story of the country club refusing to allow the Bernsteins to join. The camera showed the children walking up and down the street in front of the club. Then Susie and Bennett were being interviewed. The reporter asked Susie, "What made you think of doing this for your friend?"

Susie watched the TV screen as she saw herself answer the reporter's question. As the camera showed the crowd that had gathered around the protesters, Susie thought she saw a familiar face. There in the background was a tall and stately woman who looked just like Mrs. Roosevelt. But of course it could not possibly have been her...or could it? At this point, Susie believed anything was possible.

Susie looked at the reporter and said, "I studied Eleanor Roosevelt in school this month and learned a lot about discrimination and bravery. She was a woman who was ahead of her time. She talked about things and did things that no other woman had ever done before.

"Mrs. Roosevelt was not just our First Lady...she was the First Lady of the world. Did you know that she got nations from all over the world to support a declaration that said 'all human beings deserve all human rights'? That includes my friend, Lois Bernstein, and her family."

When the story was over, the whole family cheered. And then the phone started to ring. The first person to call was Granny Ella. Oh boy, was she proud of Susie and Bennett!

The phone continued to ring for the next hour. Everyone called to congratulate the children on the action they had taken. By seven thirty, the whole family was exhausted from all the excitement.

CHAPTER TWENTY

A Story for Bennett

Susie's legs were so tired she could barely make it up the stairs to her room. She took a bath to calm herself down and then got into bed. Her mind was racing, and she knew she would never be able to fall asleep. So she reached into the drawer of her nightstand and took out the book Aunt Linda and Uncle Bill gave her last week for her birthday.

Susie had just finished reading the first chapter when she heard someone knocking on her bedroom door. "Who's there?"

Her brother, Bennett, answered, "It's me. Can I come in for a minute?"

Susie thought his voice sounded shaky, like he might have been crying. "Sure, Bennett. Come on in. Are you OK? You look so sad."

"With all of the excitement today, I forgot about my own problem. But now I can't stop thinking about something. I really need your help. You know how Dad says, 'Sometimes life throws you a curve ball'? Well, my problem really is about curve balls!"

"What's up, Bennett?" Susie asked.

"They just announced tryouts for T-ball will be on March twelfth. All those months after the accident when I couldn't walk, you know how I did all those exercises to build up the muscles in my arms so I could use my crutches? Well, now I can throw a baseball further and faster than anyone in my class. And I can really hit the ball harder and farther than the other kids too, even kids older than me. The problem is, I still can't run very fast. So when I get a hit, it's hard for me to make it around the bases. The worst thing about it is Carl Tracker, the biggest bully in our class, will be trying out for the team. He is always teasing me. He calls me 'gimpy' and tells me to 'take a slow boat to China.' I just don't know if I can take it if he starts to make fun of me. What should I do?"

Susie thought for a moment and had an idea. She picked up the book she had just started reading and said to her little brother, "Come get into the other bed, and I will read you a story about someone else who wanted to be an athlete and had to face a lot of teasing too. Maybe it will give us some good ideas."

As his sister started to read to him from her bed, Bennett noticed that Susie still had on her red shoes. "Susie, you better take off your shoesies before you fall asleep with them on," he reminded her.

"Thanks, kiddo, I will," she replied. But Susie decided to keep them on just a little longer. They reminded her of Granny Ella, and right now, she really missed her.

Susie had only read the first few pages of her new book when she noticed that Bennett was falling asleep. She quietly reached over and turned off the lamp on the nightstand. "Don't worry, little brother," she whispered. "We'll read some more before the tryouts."

Bennett did not hear what his sister had said. He was already fast asleep. The last thing he remembered was the red glow from Susie's red shoes. It felt warm and peaceful being there with his big sister nearby. He was just about to remind her again that she still had her shoes on when he drifted off to sleep.

Susie could hear her brother's gentle breathing. She was glad he was able to forget his problems for the moment and get some much-needed sleep. The serene glow from her granny's shoes was still lighting up her bedroom, and that glow gave Susie a sense of peace and well-being. Although she did not want to take them off, Susie knew she needed her sleep too…and something told her she would need to slip out of her granny's special gift for that to happen.

Granny's Chewy, Gooey, Dark Chocolate Fudge Cake

Ingrediants:

1 stick unsalted margarine
1 cup white sugar
4 eggs, lightly beaten
1, 16-ounce can Hershey's© Syrup
1 teaspoon Baking Powder
1 teaspoon Vanilla
1 cup of Flour

Directions:

1. Place a rack in the middle of the oven, and preheat it to 325°F.
2. Bring the margarine to room temperature and cream with sugar.
3. Slowly add the lightly beaten eggs to the sugar-and-margarine mixture.
4. Slowly add the entire can of chocolate syrup.
5. Add the vanilla.
6. Make sure there are no lumps in the baking powder and add to the cake batter.
7. Slowly add the flour to the batter.
8. Use a tube pan and thoroughly grease all inside surfaces with margarine and then dust with flour. This will keep the cake from sticking to the pan.
9. Pour the batter evenly into the pan and bake for sixty minutes or until the top of the cake springs back

when touched and the cake starts to pull away from the sides of the pan. Do not overcook. After all, the cake should be chewy and gooey!

10. When the cake cools, run a knife around the edges of the pan, turn the pan over a plate, and gently tap. When the cake is cool and ready to be served, sprinkle it with powdered sugar.

To Learn More About Eleanor Roosevelt

Susie's Shoesies is historical fiction. That means, while many of the events and quotes are true, some are not. The author has tried to imagine what the historical characters might have said, if they really had been involved in the magical moments of the book.

The following books will provide you with more information about the life and times of Eleanor Roosevelt. Although some are written for adults (these are marked with an *), you probably can ask your teacher, parent, or older brother or sister to help you read the material.

Books About Eleanor Roosevelt

Cook, B. W. *Eleanor Roosevelt: Volume One, 1884–1933*. New York: Viking Press, 1992.*

———. *Eleanor Roosevelt: The Defining Years, 1933–1938*. New York: Viking Press, 1999.*

Goodwin, D. K. *No Ordinary Time: Franklin and Eleanor Roosevelt: The Home Front in World War II*. New York: Simon & Schuster, 1994.*

Freedman, R. *Eleanor Roosevelt: A Life of Discovery*. New York: Clarion Books, 1993.

Lash, J. P. *Eleanor and Franklin*. New York: Signet Press, 1971.*

Thompson, G. and N. Harrison. *Who Was Eleanor Roosevelt?* New York: Grosset & Dunlap, 2004.

Weil, A. *Eleanor Roosevelt: Fighter for Social Justice* (Childhood of Famous Americans). New York: Aladdin Paperbacks, 1989.

Books by Eleanor Roosevelt

Roosevelt, Eleanor. *This I Remember*. New York: Harper, 1949.*

———. *Ladies of Courage*. New York: Putnam, 1954.*

———. *On My Own*. New York: Harper, 1958.

———. *The Autobiography of Eleanor Roosevelt*. New York: Harper, 1961.*

Before Reading Chapter One:

1. What does the cover of _Susie's Shoesies_ make you think the story is about?
2. Where do you think the story takes place?
3. Who does most of the cooking in your family?
4. Name something that smelled really good while it was cooking in your house.
5. Who was the last visitor to come and stay at your house?
6. Do you have a bedroom all to yourself, or does someone share your room with you?
7. Do you like to have sleepovers?

Word Play for Chapter One:

Why are these words grouped together? How are they the same, and how are they different?

they're	Susie's
there	shoesies
there	Gettysburg
hair	Pittsburgh
care	
dare	
fair	

Here are some word-wall words for now and future reference. What smaller words do you see within some of these words that can help you remember how to read them and spell them in the future? Do you know the difference between an "open" and a "closed" syllable? Can you find an example of each in one of these words?

extraordinary   inspired
confirming   glimpse
lafayette   Kiev, Russia
remarkable   relationship

During Reading Chapter One:

1. How old will Granny Ella be on her next birthday?
2. In what country was Granny Ella born?
3. What was life at home like for Granny Ella when she was a child?

After Reading Chapter One:

1. Did any members of your family come to America by boat?
2. How many days did it take the boat to bring Granny Ella to America?
3. Where did Granny Ella's father settle when he came to America?
4. What does the phrase "wise beyond their young years" mean?

Before Reading Chapter Two:

1. Do you have any brothers or sisters and, if so, with whom do you play the most?
2. Can you be great friends with someone and, at the same time, also get into disagreements with him or her?
3. Has anyone in your family had a serious accident or illness, and if so, how did you feel when you found out about it?
4. What is the most special birthday present you have ever gotten?

Word Play for Chapter Two:

Why are these words grouped together? How are they the same and how are they different?

to	too
chew	threw
gooey	moon
breath	breathe
look	cook
	two
	through
	food

Here are some word-wall words for now and future reference. What smaller words do you see within some of these words that can help you remember how to read them and spell them in the future? Can you label any "open" and "closed" syllables?

emotional	sequins
unexpected	comedian
confident	electrified
protectively	nightstand
seamstress	delicious
quizzically	therapy

During Reading Chapter Two:

1. How old was Susie's brother?
2. What was the name of the Gardner family's dog?
3. How would you feel if someone in your family was getting all of the attention?
4. Why was Susie's mother so proud of her?

After Reading Chapter Two:

1. Why did Bennett think there was a fire in Susie's room?
2. Where did Granny Ella get the present she gave Susie?
3. Why did Granny Ella and Susie's mom have tears in their eyes?
4. What does the phrase "...will never fade from your heart" mean?

Before Reading Chapter Three:

1. What are some of the things you have talked to your grandmother about?
2. Have you ever had to write a report or give a presentation in school about a famous person, and if so, whom did you study?
3. Do you have any pictures of members of your family in your room?
4. Have you ever traveled to a foreign country and, if so, where?

Word Play for Chapter Three:

Why are these words grouped together? How are they the same and how are they different?

burning	turning
nurse	curse
worse	learning

Here are some word-wall words for now and future reference. What smaller words do you see within some of these words that can help you remember how to read them and spell them in the future? Can you label any "open" and "closed" syllables?

discrimination	comforting
convictions	sweetheart
inferior	famous
accomplish	statue
Philadelphia	revolution
	promise

During Reading Chapter Three:

1. About whom did Susie write her school report?
2. What does the word "discrimination" mean?
3. Whom did Granny Ella hear speaking in Paris, France, in 1948?
4. In what sport is Susie really talented?

After Reading Chapter Three:

1. Have you ever felt inferior to someone else?
2. Who were the "founding fathers" of our country?
3. What did Eleanor Roosevelt mean when she said, "It's better to light a candle than to curse the darkness?"
4. What does it mean to "resign" from an organization?
5. What do you think will happen after Susie falls asleep?

Before Reading Chapter Four:

1. Talk about a dream you once had that felt very, very real.
2. Who are your favorite singers and actors?
3. Describe your bedroom.

Word Play for Chapter Four:

Why are these words grouped together? How are they the same and how are they different?

pool	tool
received	believed
bed	said
rule	cool
instead	leave

Here are some word-wall words for now and future reference. What smaller words do you see within some of these words that can help you remember how to read them and spell them in the future? Can you label any "open" and "closed" syllables?

ceiling	membership
openings	remarkable
noticed	library
obvious	courage

During Reading Chapter Four:

1. Have you ever been to the White House?
2. What is the title of the president's wife?
3. Who are two of Susie's favorite stars?
4. What was happening to Susie's friend's family that upset her?
5. If you could go back in time, what event would you hope to visit?

After Reading Chapter Four:

1. How did Harry Truman become president?
2. How would you feel if you had the chance to meet a First Lady?
3. What would you do if one of your friends were being discriminated against?
4. Why do you think Mrs. Roosevelt was so friendly with the Trumans?
5. Where do you think the meeting Susie and Mrs. Roosevelt are going to is being held?
6. Do you think Susie really is visiting Eleanor Roosevelt? Why or why not?

Before Reading Chapter Five:

1. Have you ever been inside a limousine or antique car, and if so, what was it like?
2. What newspapers and magazines does your family read?
3. Have you ever been on a train or airplane, and if so, to where did you travel?
4. What do you know about the United Nations?

Word Play for Chapter Five:

Why are these words grouped together? How are they the same and how are they different?

rain	train
four	for
woke	broke
other	brother
boot	suit
plane	pain
crane	before
tour	oak
door	bother
soak	suitcase

Here are some word-wall words for now and future reference. What smaller words do you see within some of these words that can help you remember how to read them and spell them in the future? Can you label any "open" and "closed" syllables?

confusing   bothering

assembly   California

motorcycles   overwhelmed

enormous   instincts

During Reading Chapter Five:

1. Why were there cars in front and behind Mrs. Roosevelt's car?
2. Why were people waving at Mrs. Roosevelt's car?
3. Why would Susie and Mrs. Roosevelt need to take a plane?

After Reading Chapter Five:

1. Have you ever been excited and scared at the same time? When?
2. Across what ocean did Susie and Mrs. Roosevelt's plane have to fly?
3. What do you think Susie's family thought of all this?
4. What did Granny Ella mean when she wrote to Susie and said, "Trust your heart"?

Before Reading Chapter Six:

1. Name some different types of planes that you have seen or read about.
2. Have you ever been to a sleepover?
3. Are palaces real, or do they only exist in fairy tales?

Word Play for Chapter Six:

Why are these words grouped together? How are they the same and how are they different?

see	sleep
leap	tea
white	site
vain	train
lane	cane
Wright brothers	keep
Pain	night
Plane	stain
plain	

Here are some word-wall words for now and future reference. What smaller words do you see within some of these words that can help you remember how to read them and spell them in the future? Can you label any "open" and "closed" syllables?

dignity	delegation
equality	propellers
countries	commission
attention	apparently
princess	overwhelmed

During Reading Chapter Six:

1. What color was the plane Susie was going on?
2. What is a "delegation"?
3. Why did Mrs. Roosevelt feel the invention of the airplane had such an impact on the outcome of World War II?

After Reading Chapter Six:

1. What is the name of the document that guarantees human rights in America?
2. When was the last time you were proud of someone you knew?
3. Why does Mrs. Roosevelt tell Susie that human rights begin "close to home"?

Before Reading Chapter Seven:

1. Has the wind ever blown your hat off and, if so, when?
2. What does the presidential seal look like?
3. What is your favorite thing to eat in a restaurant?
4. Who invented French fries?

Word Play for Chapter Seven:

Why are these words grouped together? How are they the same and how are they different?

dream	cream
born	corn
rain	drain
team	seem
mourn	torn

Here are some word-wall words for now and future reference. What smaller words do you see within some of these words that can help you remember how to read them and spell them in the future? Can you label any "open" and "closed" syllables?

emblem	towels
hangar	delicious
pressure	approached
sensation	rejoin

During Reading Chapter Seven:

1. Who do you think is going to share the bedroom with Susie?
2. What did Susie order for dinner the first night on the plane?
3. Why did Susie feel pressure in her ears?

After Reading Chapter Seven:

1. Why did they turn off the lights in the cabin?
2. Why were they celebrating Susie's birthday the night before?
3. Why did Susie say, "I feel like pinching myself"?
4. Why is Susie afraid that this may all just be a dream?

Before Reading Chapter Eight:

1. What do you know about Franklin Roosevelt?
2. Have you ever had to give a speech to a large group of people, and if so, how did it make you feel?
3. Have you ever gone along with your parents when they voted?
4. How would you feel if a law was passed that said, "People with blond hair are not allowed to vote anymore"?

Word Play for Chapter Eight:

Why are these words grouped together? How are they the same and how are they different?

wear	dear
bear	fear
beat	meat
bee	meet
share	sharing
care	caring

Here are some word-wall words for now and future reference. What smaller words do you see within some of these words that can help you remember how to read them and spell them in the future? Can you label any "open" and "closed" syllables?

religion	childhood
suffered	protested
foreign	criticized
bedspread	embarrassment

suffragettes   expression
superficial   diphtheria
journey   nervous

During Reading Chapter Eight:

1. What does "Children should be seen and not heard" mean?
2. What do Susie's granny and Mrs. Roosevelt have in common?
3. What were the women called who protested that women did not have equal rights?

After Reading Chapter Eight:

1. Where did Eleanor Roosevelt spend most of her high school days?
2. Was Mrs. Roosevelt's family rich or poor, and how did she feel about it?
3. Why was Franklin Roosevelt proud of his wife?

Before Reading Chapter Nine:

1. What is your favorite thing to have for breakfast?
2. What is your favorite thing to wear to a fancy occasion?
3. What is the name of the most beautiful building you have ever seen?
4. Have you ever worn something that was "passed down" to you or was borrowed and, if so, what did you think of that?

Word Play for Chapter Nine:

Why are these words grouped together? How are they the same and how are they different?

rise	surprise
treat	sweet
first	burst
ties	prize
feet	prize
	heat
	worst

Here are some word-wall words for now and future reference. What smaller words do you see within some of these words that can help you remember how to read them and spell them in the future? Can you label any "open" and "closed" syllables?

gentle	photographers
security	prepared
glistened	prepared

outfit   opportunity
disappoint   brilliant
gorgeous   community
                        statues

During Reading Chapter Nine:

1. What did Susie think of the outfit Mrs. Roosevelt picked out for her?
2. How old was Susie when Eleanor Roosevelt said, "Happy birthday, sweetheart"?
3. How did Mrs. Roosevelt describe Susie to the photographers?

After Reading Chapter Nine:

1. Why did Mrs. Roosevelt think this trip would help Susie's hometown?
2. Why do you think the outfit Eleanor Roosevelt chose for Susie was red, white, and blue?
3. Why did the American delegation need airport security?
4. Did Susie wear her new shoes to the palace? Why or why not?

Before Reading Chapter Ten:

1. What were some terrible things that happened in World War II?
2. Do you speak a foreign language, and if so, when have you used it?
3. Do you have any chandeliers in your house?
4. What do you think the inside of a palace looks like?

Word Play for Chapter Ten:

Why are these words grouped together? How are they the same and how are they different?

most	host
healing	ceiling
roast	coast
kneeling	feeling

Here are some word-wall words for now and future reference. What smaller words do you see within some of these words that can help you remember how to read them and spell them in the future? Can you label any "open" and "closed" syllables?

enormous	embroidered
chandeliers	rainbows
crystal	foreign
empire	damage
declaration	converse
witness	

During Reading Chapter Ten:

1. Who appointed Eleanor Roosevelt to the United Nations delegation and why?
2. When sunlight shone on the chandeliers, what happened?
3. What year did Franklin Roosevelt die?
4. What does the term "allied nations" mean?

After Reading Chapter Ten:

1. Why were so many flags hanging from the walls of the meeting room?
2. For whom do you think the two golden chairs were made?
3. What prepared Mrs. Roosevelt for speaking in front of an international audience?

Before Reading Chapter Eleven:

1. In what ways do different governments treat their citizens differently?
2. What does the word "civilized" mean to you?
3. Have you ever been to an event held in a ballroom and, if so, when?
4. Have you ever been to a restaurant where they had a buffet, and if so, what was your favorite thing to eat?

Word Play for Chapter Eleven:

Why are these words grouped together? How are they the same and how are they different?

fire	tire
phone	tone
own	away
buffet	inspire

Here are some word-wall words for now and future reference. What smaller words do you see within some of these words that can help you remember how to read them and spell them in the future? Can you label any "open" and "closed" syllables?

hopeful	denying
anxious	audience
patiently	protective
applauded	escorted
entitled	keyhole
thunderous	elegance

conscious   responsibility
imperfections   podium

During Reading Chapter Eleven:

1. Did the delegates like Mrs. Roosevelt's speech?
2. Why was the ceiling of the ballroom painted blue?
3. Why did Mrs. Roosevelt ask the French delegates to speak English, even though she spoke fluent French?

After Reading Chapter Eleven:

1. Why would a country *not* want to sign the declaration?
2. Why did the delegate refer to Mrs. Roosevelt as "the First Lady of the world"?
3. Do you believe that people should be treated equally, and if so, why?

Before Reading Chapter Twelve:

1. What is your favorite dessert?
2. What does the word "gooey" mean?
3. Have you or your family ever asked someone to share a recipe and, if so, for what dish?
4. Have you ever seen a restaurant kitchen and, if so, when and where?

Word Play for Chapter Twelve:

Why are these words grouped together? How are they the same and how are they different?

her	bird
serve	heard
mile	dial
file	trial
brave	cave

Here are some word-wall words for now and future reference. What smaller words do you see within some of these words that can help you remember how to read them and spell them in the future? Can you label any "open" and "closed" syllables?

overheard	storage
whisper	knob
envelope	figure
confident	spiral
accomplished	

During Reading Chapter Twelve:

1. Were the people at her table upset with her when Susie asked for a second piece of dessert? Why or why not?
2. Where had Susie had a similar dessert?
3. Why did Mrs. Roosevelt ask Betty to go with Susie to tour the kitchen?

After Reading Chapter Twelve:

1. How could the chef at the Palais de Chaillot have made the same cake as Susie's granny?
2. Who asked for the cake recipe and why?
3. How do you think Susie and Betty will get out of the storage room?

Before Reading Chapter Thirteen:

1. What have you been taught to do in case of a fire?
2. Did you ever get lost, and if so, when and where did this happen?
3. How did you find your way?
4. Did anyone notice that you were missing or lost?

Word Play for Chapter Thirteen:

Why are these words grouped together? How are they the same, and how are they different?

succeed	proceed
greed	freed
lead	read
bread	leave

Here are some word-wall words for now and future reference. What smaller words do you see within some of these words that can help you remember how to read them and spell them in the future? Can you label any "open" and "closed" syllables?

disrupted	suspicious
pantry	twine
medicine	ankles
succeeded	conquering
paperweight	

During Reading Chapter Thirteen:

1. What did Susie mean when she said Eleanor Roosevelt was her "role model"?
2. Why were the telephone wires cut?
3. Why did Betty wink at Susie?

After Reading Chapter Thirteen:

1. Why did the kidnapper go back to the ballroom?
2. Did he really care about Susie and Betty?
3. Why did the light coming in under the door remind Susie of her brother?
4. How do you think Susie and Betty will get out of the office?

Before Reading Chapter Fourteen:

1. Has anyone ever stolen anything from you or your family and, if so, when and where?
2. Should all people who are caught stealing be treated the same?
3. Why would someone steal from someone else?
4. What things do you do to make sure your possessions are safe?

Word Play for Chapter Fourteen:

Why are these words grouped together? How are they the same and how are they different?

law	flaw
steal	deal
gnaw	claw
wheel	

Here are some word-wall words for now and future reference. What smaller words do you see within some of these words that can help you remember how to read them and spell them in the future? Can you label any "open" and "closed" syllables?

approached	illegally
progressing	abandoned
treatment	rescued
humanely	tugging
prison	

During Reading Chapter Fourteen:

1. What were the two kidnappers' names?
2. Why did Betty pretend to have a heart attack?
3. Was the declaration going to be a law?

After Reading Chapter Fourteen:

1. What is the difference between a statement of principles and a law?
2. Why did Susie ask Betty to turn off the light?
3. Why did the rescuers break down the door to the office?
4. In what ways were Susie and Betty smart?
5. In what ways were Susie and Betty brave?
6. What did Mrs. Roosevelt mean by "a good faith effort"?

Before Reading Chapter Fifteen:

1. Why do people gather to see famous people?
2. Have you ever seen or heard a famous person give a speech?
3. If you could meet a famous person, whom would you like it to be…and why?

Word Play for Chapter Fifteen:

Why are these words grouped together? How are they the same and how are they different?

out	about
cloud	loud
older	shoulder
dim	him
climb	limb
hymn	crowd

Here are some word-wall words for now and future reference. What smaller words do you see within some of these words that can help you remember how to read them and spell them in the future? Can you label any "open" and "closed" syllables?

familiar	distinguished
shocked	whispered
approached	eventually

During Reading Chapter Fifteen:

1. Whom did Susie think she saw outside the Palais de Chaillot?
2. What made Susie think she knew this person?
3. Why was Susie surprised at the name of the cake?

After Reading Chapter Fifteen:

1. What was the name of the recipe?
2. What was surprising about the way it was written?
3. Where else in the story did you read about a woman having her picture taken in Paris?

Before Reading Chapter Sixteen:

1. When was the last time you were away from home without your family?
2. Did you miss them the whole time you were away or just during certain times?
3. Can you think of something you did that made your parents proud?

Word Play for Chapter Sixteen:

Why are these words grouped together? How are they the same and how are they different?

calm	balm
thought	palm
caught	bought
taught	paused

Here are some word-wall words for now and future reference. What smaller words do you see within some of these words that can help you remember how to read them and spell them in the future? Can you label any "open" and "closed" syllables?

glimpses	instincts
witness	communities
aglow	presidential
sparkled	electrified

During Reading Chapter Sixteen:

1. Why is Paris called the "City of Lights"?
2. Was Susie proud of Mrs. Roosevelt and, if so, why?
3. What did Susie do when she got back to the plane?

After Reading Chapter Sixteen:

1. Was the meeting at the Palais de Chaillot successful? Why or why not?
2. What was the last thing Susie did before she went to bed on the airplane?
3. What do you think will happen when Susie wakes up?
4. How do you think what Susie saw and learned in Paris will affect her life in Pennsylvania?

Before Reading Chapter Seventeen:

1. Do you know anyone else who has the same birthday as you and, if so, what is that like for you?
2. If you could get anything you want for your next birthday, what would that be?
3. Do you have your own computer, or do you share one with the rest of your family?

Word Play for Chapter Seventeen:

Why are these words grouped together? How are they the same, and how are they different?

ears	fears
cheers	snow
know	toes
froze	hears
grow	blow
	nose

Here are some word-wall words for now and future reference. What smaller words do you see within some of these words that can help you remember how to read them and spell them in the future? Can you label any "open" and "closed" syllables?

laptop	thorns
argue	research
Wilma Rudolph	determination
spunk	

During Reading Chapter Seventeen:

1. Why did Susie think Bennett gave her the perfect present?
2. Why was Susie so excited about the present her parents gave her?
3. Why was Granny Ella so excited about her birthday present?

After Reading Chapter Seventeen:

1. Whom do you think Granny Ella will take with her to Paris?
2. Will this be Granny Ella's first trip to Paris? What makes you think it is or is not?
3. Who did Susie think gave her the nightgown and robe?
4. Who was Wilma Rudolph and why did Susie's aunt and uncle choose the book they did?

Before Reading Chapter Eighteen:

1. Have you ever misplaced something and then found it in a strange place?
2. Have you ever seen a picket line? What were the people protesting?
3. Have you ever been to your local town hall? If so, why?
4. How often do you get to see your grandparents?

Word Play for Chapter Eighteen:

Why are these words grouped together? How are they the same, and how are they different?

bored	board
floor	roared
chord	happy
happier	

Here are some word-wall words for now and future reference. What smaller words do you see within some of these words that can help you remember how to read them and spell them in the future? Can you label any "open" and "closed" syllables?

especially	index
darkness	recipes
celebrity	referring
announced	resigning
auction	situation
picket	protest
manager	membership

During Reading Chapter Eighteen:

1. Where did Granny Ella get the cake recipe?
2. What was the name of Susie's friend's family who was denied membership by the country club?
3. What was one of Susie's family's favorite things to have for lunch?
4. What did Susie think they should do to help their friends?

After Reading Chapter Eighteen:

1. Did Susie tell her mother or grandmother what happened in Paris? Why or why not?
2. How can picketing a business cause people to change their minds about a decision they made?
3. What did Susie mean when she said, "If we make the news"?

Before Reading Chapter Nineteen:

1. Do you ever watch the news? If so, why?
2. What is a silent auction?
3. Can children be effective when they stand up for what is right and, if so, in what ways?

Word Play for Chapter Nineteen:

Why are these words grouped together? How are they the same and how are they different?

fired	tired
few	news
weird	wired
use	clues
fuse	

Here are some word-wall words for now and future reference. What smaller words do you see within some of these words that can help you remember how to read them and spell them in the future? Can you label any "open" and "closed" syllables?

permit	youngest
morning	protester
importantly	congratulations
permit	exhausted
waiters	slogan
deserve	commotion

During Reading Chapter Nineteen:

1. What was the slogan Bennett thought of for the picketing signs and why was it typical for him to think of this phrase?
2. Where did everyone go for lunch after the golf tournament, and why?
3. What did Susie tell the reporter inspired her to take this action?

After Reading Chapter Nineteen:

1. Why does the phone at Susie's house keep ringing all night?
2. Who was the first person to call Susie?
3. How did Susie's family feel at the end of the day, and why?
4. How do you think Mr. Gage felt at the end of the day?

Before Reading Chapter Twenty:

1. What do you do when you are really exhausted and need to relax?
2. Whom do you confide in when you have a problem?
3. Who confides in you when he or she has a problem?
4. What is your favorite sport to play?

Word Play for Chapter Twenty:

Why are these words grouped together? How are they the same, and how are they different?

shake
shaky
flake
flaky

Here are some word-wall words for now and future reference. What smaller words do you see within some of these words that can help you remember how to read them and spell them in the future? Can you label any "open" and "closed" syllables?

exercises	knocking
curve	drawer
moment	athlete
muscles	nearby

During Reading Chapter Twenty:

1. What sport did Bennett want to play?
2. Was he confident in his sports ability? Why or why not?
3. Where did Susie get the book she started to read to her brother?

After Reading Chapter Twenty:

1. Why did Susie decide to take off her shoes before going to bed? Was that a good idea and if so, why?
2. What do you think would have happened if she had left them on?
3. Have you ever had a dream that came true, and if so, what was it?

Acknowledgements

This book would not be possible without the love and support of my family and friends. To Stan Levine, Lois Baron, Sandy Idstein, Beve Kraut, and Sally Magen Brown, who read the manuscript in its earliest stages, thank you for your enthusiasm and editorial comments.

To Lori, Alex, and Erica, thank you for listening to book readings and enjoying cake eating and game playing.

To the teachers, librarians, and students at Wilmington Friends Lower School, the Academy in Manayunk, and the Tatnall Lower School, thank you for allowing me to do book readings and giving me your attention and opinions.

Lastly, to Jenny, Kayla, and my creative team, thank you for taking good care of Susie and me. You made sure the world saw and heard the characters I created as I wanted them to be remembered. Next time, at the Olympics!

About the Author

Sue Madway Levine has been working with children, families, and schools for more than forty years. As a speech and language therapist, learning disabilities resource teacher, college professor, researcher, and published author, Sue has dedicated her professional life to making a positive difference in the field of education. During her work at Dominican University in San Rafael, CA, Sue hosted game-making workshops for local teachers. This led to her working in the toy and game industry, inventing new products for companies such as Parker Brothers, Milton Bradley, Hasbro, Mattel, Pressman Toy Company, Tiger Electronics, and The Great American Puzzle Factory. After having two of her textbooks published by Academic Therapy Publishing, Sue has now turned to writing children's literature. Presently, she is in private practice as the Director of Educational Services for the Child and Family Study Team. She lives in a suburb of Philadelphia, PA, with her husband, a service learning coordinator at a local school district. Sue spends her free time gardening and traveling. If you would like more information about Sue or *Susie's Shoesies*, such as watching chapter readings or a lesson on how to bake a chewy, gooey, dark chocolate fudge cake, please go to www.SusiesShoesies.com.

Made in the USA
Middletown, DE
30 June 2016